High-Mount's Champion

Raymond Herrera

Copyright © 2024 by Raymond Herrera

All rights reserved.

No portion of this book may be reproduced in any form without written permission from the publisher or author, except as permitted by U.S. copyright law.

— · —

For the Lord Jesus Christ, His Church, my Family and Friends.
Who taught me to love life and to love a good story.

CONTENTS

PROLOGUE

A Champion's call is one that many will not answer.

But one answer came from an unlikely source.
Only to face a journey filled with Faith,
betrayal, monsters, and the undead.
The story you are about to find here began long ago.
In a time when kings and queens
remained rulers of the land,
knights and grand warriors fought in battles of old.
Where the supernatural and monsters
remained roaming around the land,
once lived the Kingdom of High-Mount.
The landscape was lavish and green
with vegetation far and wide, emerald and fresh!
The forests and fields were rampant with much life.
Then there were mountains and swamps
at its their highest and lowest,
dark and dangerous were these for travelers.
No one would dare venture near the one mountain.
For in it lie a grim and terrible secret
that was waiting to reveal itself to the world.

In the midst of that forest near the capital.
Beyond the grainfields and off the main roads.

The One who has created.
Who created sea and land.
Yet it was Him they hated.
Yet their words are sand.

There were a few kingdoms spread
throughout the World.
Some were to the north and to the south,
others were from the east to the west.
Although a majority of these powerful kingdoms
were to the east and to the north,
none of them were as festive and as militant
as the Kingdom of High-Mount in the southwest.
Its' own capital was a grand fortress of a city.
Filled with all kinds of markets and businesses
and shows and more!
This city was very alive and dandy!

Set up shop, you local markets!
your balances you businesses.
and actors you stage sets!
For all may access!

As for the daily lives of the citizens,
there were many who many were festive in attitude.
Some were always in a hurry here and there,

going about their day in their wagons and carts.
Some yelled at everyone for not knowing to ride!
Many attended places of foods and entertainment.
From the poetic theaters and the colosseum of sports.
To the calmest of gardens and parks.
There were also a couple of parishes in the city.
One was the Church of the Holy Ingot,
and the other was the St. Gabriel Catholic Church.
Holy Ingot was full of polished marble,
and grand jewelry and promised the people
that they will inherit wealth and health
if they believe in God.
St. Gabriel Catholic Church was a stark difference.
It looked more like a relic then anything bright.
Built from old stones, old metal.
The inside is where its beauty truly shined.
A warm and reverent presence
with its stained-glass windows
and its marble alter and ancient yet
radiant tabernacle with colorful portraits.
Sometimes you would hear the sounds of bells
and a pipe-organ playing sorrowfully at times.
Other times they would be playing
gleeful and reverent hymns during Mass.

Why this rivalry?
History vs. Money?
To some, both are mockery.
Yet one has life and not fakery.

The culture was filled with life,
filled with festive colors of reds,
yellows, greens, blues, purples, and teals.
However, the main colors of
High-Mount's flags and banners;
a range of red, gold, black, white, and purple.
Alongside these colors were also a kingdom
that was filled with all kinds of aromas.
Baked goods like pan dulce, tortillas, crepes, fritters!
Spices and peppers ranging from
nutmeg and garlics to serranoes and paprikas!
Meats from the richest of steaks, lamb, and schnitzel.
To the cheapest of barbacoa, fajitas, and bratwurst.
Around every corner, farmers sold their harvests
of potatoes, carrots, onions, beets, and turnips.
Adding to the feast with no end in sight!

Feast upon feast.
Fun upon fun
Greatest to least
All are never done!

I

—·—

THE BLACKSMITH OF HIGH-MOUNT

W ithin the walls
of Brackenridge Palace,
with all the gold, velvet, and jade,
there lived the High-Mount Royalty.
High-Mount's Princess was
known as Princess Eithne.
She was an active one for sure.
For she had fair and just causes to pursue!
Pale and freckled skinned was she.
Hair as bright as a coppery flames
with a passion for her life.
It was always a dream of hers
to help her kingdom in the way
she saw to be as best for all.
"I have seen life beyond that palace.
How the rich always get richer
and the poor always become poorer.
Why must life be this way?
I will ensure that no one suffers

in this way anymore!"

Friendship is sweet
Sweet as honey.
Like ale from wheat,
So is friendship sunny.

These thoughts she had everyday:
I have it all, yet all yet have nothing.
I am the princess yet have no power.
If I was queen, I will serve those around me
for the longevity and goodness
of my family's kingdom.
If I could just do something,
all will be good in the end.
All will know right from wrong
and do something about it!
I will someday, but will I ever?
Those like Aaron could have something.
The poor won't have to suffer so much.
The rich will be held accountable!
If only I could be crowned as Queen sooner.
Of course Eithne means well
with her ambitions and vision.
Yet, how will she go about
fulfilling them when the occasion
to do so should rise up?

Those with power,

They must do something!
Those without power,
Must they have nothing?

She and a young blacksmith
had grown up together.
Both high and low where they both stood,
yet it was no matter to them.
This blacksmith was a young man,
whose name was Aaron.
He was from a family of blacksmiths.
The youngest of three sibling.
who will meant to inherit nothing.
Raven black hair and bronze skinned,
eyes green as emerald. What a sight!
A goodly man with a heart of silver.
This blacksmith was hot-headed yet honest;
A man full of arrogance, but also with compassion.
These were his own thoughts everyday:
"I have lots of thoughts, but no one will listen!
My sisters will have everything,
but I inherit nothing!
IT'S UNFAIR, I SAY! What must I do?
I want to be someone,
do something! If I was a hero,
I could be something,
be significant to my family,
to the Kingdom.
Am I not made for more than this?

Why must I be poor?
Why must be any last?
This can't be rougher!
My life, an Outcast."

When the young princess and blacksmith
were just children who had
not a single worry in the world,
these two had a secret place.
There, they were not royalty nor worker,
they were just simply kids.
One day, when they were
merely 9 and 10 years old respectively,
they went to their secret place and
just hung out to vent their
simple yet childish experiences
of frustrations and wonders.
"How wonderful our dreams are!"
said Aaron who was filled with glee.
"How so? You can achieve your goals,
yet I am powerless to achieve
mine as I currently am."
Eithne asked while lamenting her lot.
"I'm just a blacksmith, and yet
I could be anything if I can have glory!
In fact, I could be a great hero someday..."
Aaron cried with passion and a longing
for something greater then him.

"Maybe, but you'll be ensured justice
when I become queen someday.
With my own council and army.
To fix our kingdom's problems."
Eithne assured while pompous.
Determined with holding
a make-shift scepter in hand.
They always wished that times
would be simple like their hangouts,
yet they will find a few years later.
Things, would not be so...

Some are royal.
Others are workers.
When both are loyal.
Everything is better.

Deep within the mountain in the woods,
there laid a grim and terrible secret.
Some would call it a mountain,
for it appeared to many like one.
Others believed it to bring bad omens.
For those who dared explore
were doomed to never return.
Now, there lived a warrior that
had been exiled from High-Mount
for reasons only the Royalty had known,
but would not reveal it all to the public.
But this warrior discovered something

of an unknown nature once he did find it.
To his surprise, not a mountain,
but an abandoned citadel!
Why, this was the Eckhert Citadel!
A place long lost in time
due to a history unknown.
Now it stands a relic.
Some say an ancient evil dwells in there now.
While others claim:
To be near the citadel at all
meant agonizing death regardless
if one managed to escape its dread.
Such a supernatural evil would find its prey.
Eventually, this warrior found the
creature and learned that it was
indeed a supernatural creature!
It said to the exiled vagabond:
"I know of the hardships you had to face.
You gave and you gave.
And your good was repaid for evil.
Serve me. Give yourself to me,
your body and soul, and I shall
help you take your revenge!"
The Entity bargained.
"If that is what it will take for those
pigs and sloths to end their evil,
I'll commit my whole self to you!"
he said as he knelt before the entity.
Lights and hues surrounded the warrior.

Stripping whatever humanity he
had in exchange for raw power
and a new hardened body.
"There are tasks which must be done.
We must act immediately
if we are to succeed.
When *she* is in our grasp,
we shall rise!!"

Why throw your lives away?
You vengeful and dumb bunch?
All you shall know is dismay.
Your lives gone in a rabid crunch.

Years later, on one fateful day,
with Aaron being 20 and Eithne being 19,
the city of High-Mount celebrates
The Festival of Falling Leaves which usually
falls around the 10th month of the year!
Warm colors and spices are in the air!
Many celebrate the coming of the season.
In the palace and in the streets,
from singing and dancing to buying and selling!
It was a delight to see this time of year!
Aaron and Eithne were with their families
as they celebrated this wonderous holiday!
When Eithne could just rejoice and not sit idly by,
Aaron could rejoice and not whine.
Truly, this was something to see!

Rejoice you who whine!
Rejoice you who idle!
For it is time to dine!
And to grab the seidel!

Then, the air went cold and smelled like rot.
Monsters of sludge and flesh decaying.
Perversions of nature they were!
Emerging from the rich ground.
Screams and screeches and running
went the ghouls and citizens!
Joys and fun became sorrow and chaos!
Then rising from the ground was he:
A ragged and robed figure
leads the ghoulish and
sludge-plagued undead!
A 8-foot giant in stature,
with a halberd that was
double-bladed on both ends of the shaft.
His face was wrapped in cloth,
with a singular yellow eye showing
from the right side of his face.
A majority of the Kings' knights
had fallen in battle.
But the blacksmiths and
whoever was left had decided
to take arms to defend the people!

When all all-out fails,
When all seems lost,
Valiant hearts sail!
No matter the cost.

Swords slashed! Hammer smashed!

Spears pierced! Slash!

Bash! Crash! Splash! Swish!

Aaron's family fought with all they had!

Heads and limbs and blood flew whoosh

and slash and crash! Metallic sounds

and taste of blood in the air!

Through the town and in the palace

was the plagued air flowing through

the whole town and within the palace.

They made their way to the King's Court.

With grand walls and ceilings in gold and velvet.

Stained Glass shards and blood was everywhere!

There he stood, the robed and ragged figure.

With the Princess held hostage,

the undead clenched her with their cold,

dead and slimy hands.

As for the King and Queen,

they have been trapped on their thrones with sludge.

"Let her go!" Aaron yelled yet timidly.

The figure gazed at him smugly and said,

"Then come, take her."

Then he drew his with halberd in both hands.

Eithne could only watch,

knowing the chances of Aaron's victory
being slim to null.
"What are you doing!?
Don't throw your life away like this!"
She yelled as she struggled
with the undead restraining her.

A blacksmith and a soldier.
Aaron was over his head!
Though it was to free her,
Aaron was almost dead.

Aaron charged with his sword in hand!
Only for the figure to dash and bash!
The warrior disarmed the novice blacksmith,
then knocked him down.
"How foolish you are, young blacksmith."
Proclaimed the figure with his foot over
Aaron's back and hand over his face,
pinning him to the stone floor.
"As a knight you would've
been a worthy adversary.
Yet you're reminded of your place.
For I surpass even the king!
May my name, Balaam,
haunt your to the end of your days.
Now I must be gone." Balaam concluded.
With that, he, his army, and Eithne vanished.
Aaron, weakened and beaten,

had uttered weakly to himself:
"Eithne, forgive me of my folly.
I shall save you as atonement.
You would've done the same for me."
He fainted as he reached his hand out to
Eithne before she vanished completely,
then there was silence within
the messy and ruined court.
When the battle was won
in High-Mount's favor,
the Royal family, and Aaron,
all lamenting and defeated.
The Royal family worded:

"Our daughter has vanished!
Woes be the Undead's nature!
Woe to the Traitor's banished!
Who will be her savior?"

After a week's recovery, Aaron,
feeling a great sense of indignation and
a passionate desire for vengeance,
had his strength and wits renewed,
he could have his glory and fortune.
In order to save his friend,
he requested an audience with the court.
Now, the court room itself was glamorous
as one would expect when entering
a courtroom before the king and queen.

Filled with fine and polished marble
and the finest of oak furniture of tables,
seats, facing the throne above them all.
He entered the court and proclaimed:
"I shall be your daughter's savior and slay the fiend!"
At this, the Court roared in laughter!
For the King has told the court beforehand
his side of what happened that day
prior to the present hearing.
Even the king laughed and scoffed:
"HA! My dear boy, I've seen you
lose to him! What chance are you
against a soldier from birth?
It will be a massacre if you tried!"

Our dear blacksmith,
One with a big heart.
Yet such man, a myth.
Not much, But it's a start.

"He may be a soldier, but I'm a blacksmith!
I'm more creative with what I have!
I'll just have to win once!"
Aaron argued before the court,
only for them to laugh longer and louder.
One particular Councilmember was a nobleman
who seemed to be a bit too big for his britches
(even though his clothes were thick with velvet)
which showed his wealth.

A Patron of the Church of the Holy Ingot.
He only said this to piss him off:
"Oh please young man.
You're all bark and no bite.
'more creative,' 'win once?'
THIS, is the real High-Mount, not that
heroic underdog nonsense of yours.
You gave all you got and got nothing!
Perhaps, because you're not heroic!
So quit living in fantasies, you mongrel!"

Fantasy or reality?
Either rich or poor,
it was not the decree.
It was his own valor.

This indeed was the spark for Aaron's rage,
he then sprinted to this member
And socked him in the jaw! WHAM!
Then a couple of guards had to hold Aaron down.
"¡Cállate estúpido glotón!"
Aaron yelled with the rage of a thousand saints.
"Your highness, please arrest this lunatic!"
One councilmember yelled.
"This man is a danger to the Kingdom!"
Another councilmember yelled.
Now, word got out that Aaron's family
and several others fought valiantly against the undead hoard.
The King, fearing the people would riot

if word got out that a heroic icon;
loved by the Kingdom's People, was arrested.
So, he decided to let Aaron off with a warning,
by kicking him out of the room.
"Haven't you given us enough grief?
You embarrass yourself and your own
family with your presence! Leave us!"
He demanded with tears in his eyes.
The Court laughed and yelled in a mix of
passion and humor about the situation.
Once out of the castle itself,
Aaron sulked to himself
all humiliated and angry:

"How could the King jest?
Should he know Eithne's friendships?
I could be the very best!
To prevent High-Mount's Apocalypse..."

A few days went by since that humiliation,
and High-Mount's suffering became worse.
Pieces of farmland and crops
gave off a dim and strange
variation of black with an subtle orange hue.
Some lands were deemed unapproachable.
Once they were eaten,
the food and crops from those lands
left a metallic taste in the mouth
as well as having severe fatigue.

Those who devoured the contaminated food
would develop the black and orange
substance overtime which would tear
their bodies apart until they
would slowly but surely perish.
They couldn't even bury the bodies
due to the demonic contamination,
so they cremated them.
As a result of this,
High-Mount was subject to severe famine.
Food became scarce for everyone.
The Royalty wept for their lost princess.
Aaron had fasted since the day
of his humiliation in the court.

A mysterious color,
It was everywhere!
The pure horror
no one could bear!

Aaron and his family were lucky not to fall ill.
They were, however, subject to the famine
like everyone else in the kingdom.
Adding salt to the wounds of Aaron's ego.
Work was more difficult on an
empty stomach and spiritual fasting.
Toiling away in the forge all day was a nightmare;
An unusual suffering for him
considering his family's vocation.

Though Aaron was smart to be silent,
it tore him up from within;
The thought of failing his friend.
Suffering from starvation late at night,
Aaron was cleaning the forge,
then looked and beheld,
the family forge was on fire,
with the fire being a bright purple.
The flame was giant, yet serene.
Aaron was terrified, so he looked away.
Then he looked and beheld,
the flame took the shape of a man:

"Do not be afraid!
Do you see yourself a king?
Arise and prepare to face me,
and you shall answer."

The voice boomed like that of thunder.
Aaron arose from the ground and knelt
before the figure to say:
"Lord, my friend has been captured.
I'm qualified to save her,
but the King sees me not worthy.
I know I'm not a soldier, but I am a friend!
Should that be enough?
Even when no one else will?
I mean... I have nothing to say
but that I will go on this quest either way.

If I have sinned against you,
then I pray for your mercy.
Whatever I gain through this quest,
I shall give back to you as thanks.
You asked to present myself to you,
so I did!"

You humble, fight the good fight!
You prideful, lower yourselves!
Then you shall walk as in daylight!
One day, all shall reveal themselves.

Upon this, the figure said to Aaron
with a hand offered to him, firmly yet gently:
"Aaron, Aaron, have you forgot
that your sins are forgiven?
This nation has forgotten me.
But I have a few who still know me,
and I remember them.
For they are my sheep.
They know me and I know them.
Which is why, I am sending you.
Through you, High-Mount will
know my name once again and call upon me.
I am with you even to the end of the World."
Upon hearing these words of encouragement,
Aaron felt a sense of peace as he proclaimed:
"You humble the proud and exalt the humble.
Blessed be the name of the LORD!"

Joyful are those whose sins are forgiven,
Whose salvation gives them new life.
New-life are dead-hearts given.
A redemption towards everlasting life.

With that proclamation,
the flame dispersed everywhere.
Consuming the workshop in a purple flame!
Yet everything was left unharmed.
The workshop now smelled like Frankincense.
Then Aaron heard a gentle whisper:
"I will never leave you nor forsake you."
Where the flame once stood,
a small rose bush had now taken its place.
Aaron took a rose from the humble little bush.
Such an encounter filled him with a great vigor.
With this, he got up and ran to the Church.
Once there, he knocked on the door in the gate
for hope of an audience with the priest and clergy.
He presented the message to the clergy, proclaiming:

"I have with me a rose!
A rose from the Lord Himself!
I have seen Him face-to-face!
I have seen him myself!"

The Priest, whose name was Father Luke,
was groggy from sleep,

only to see the rose in a famine.
With this he responded weakly:
"How can this be?
How can one see the LORD and still live?"
Aaron responded: "It was a vision, I tell you!
He was a purple fire and promised to be with me!
"Surely, this message be true!
How can a rose bloom in this famine?
Has He answered our prayers?
Perhaps a champion?"
Aaron was now feeling a bit puffy
thinking that God appeared to him
out of all people to do His Will, told Father Luke:
"Yes! I shall be that champion!"
"Are you sure this is what
our Lord has called you to do?
Then tell me everything."
A couple of hours went by,
and Aaron told the Clergy
all that had happened in the workshop.
The divine presence and message exactly.
"God be praised!
He has made himself known in our hour of need!
Could you be our new champion?"

How great to be heard!
For they will find peace!
No more the mind blurred!
May the torment cease...

"I wanted to bring the good news to you.
To know that God is with us even if everyone
else has forgotten Him!"
Aaron proclaimed with glee in his eyes.
The priest was still a little slow from
sleep, though he did say:
"Yes... He has made Himself known.
If you truly are His new Champion,
then perhaps the Arch-wings will choose you."
"Wait, hold on a minute, Arch-wings?"
Aaron wondered with a sense of curiously.
"Yes, there have been legends about a pair of wings
that would find the champion,
If he is worthy, he can soar like that of an angel
and have strength like that of the Behemoth itself.
But be warned, young man.
For there was once one who abused its power.
He then became consumed with his own
pride and bloodlust, and I hope to spare you of that.
Now go in peace, glorifying the LORD with your life."
The Priest explained and then blessed Aaron.
This, of course, filled Aaron's curiosity and ego.
Surely, I am worthy of these wings...
I can't be like the one before me if they
fell from grace. I just want glory and fortune.
Not as one above everyone as a king.
Aaron thought while seeing himself out.

A man to go on a quest.
Courageous and bold.
What could this be but a test?
Surely this tale be told!

Aaron had prepared himself for this grand quest:
His standard clothes with a white cloak,
held with a broach of the family crest.
A blue gambeson with plate armor for the chest
and the back, a pair of pauldrons for his shoulders,
and grieves for his legs.
A kettle helm that was modified with a faceplate,
As well as a ration of food and tools.
Though the food was not much,
it was enough for a day's journey or two.
Finally, for his weapons he had equipped
a black and silver heater shield and his
blessed sword he deemed "Caelestis"
for God in Heaven was watching over him.
Most of these were stored in a backpack
that was patched with many
pouches for a lot of storage.
Now this is a look fit for a hero!
Aaron thought to himself.
This whole quest he dared to go on,
he hoped that this glorious and redemptive
quest be blessed by the LORD God Himself.
But little did this young man know.
Of the hills and valleys he will

endure the next couple of days...
the prideful yet kind-hearted fool...

Armored and packed is he
Young Aaron who is Icarus.
Where will the Princess be?
Within Apollyon's' Abyss?

2

—·—

THE UNEXPECTED ALLIANCE

Princess Eithne was awakened and fatigued.

She found herself in a dark room with a
subtle orange hue that appeared here and there.
Appering all over each wall that which was
filled with stained-glass windows
of a familiar history to the Princess.
Next to a throne, caged in a ghastly box.
Wha- where am I? What is this? She thought.
She tried to punch it, then it pushed her back.
"Argh!" She yelled, stunned by the recoil.
Then a figure emerging from within the darkness.
"Don't bother, your cage is of my creation. "
He told her coldly and broodingly.
"That voice... Show yourself!" Eithne yelled.
"You should know who I am, Princess.
Your captor is also your savior."
He responded as he emerged from the shadows.

Where is the Princess?

What trickery is this?
All there remains is darkness.
Is her life now gone, dismiss?

"You... the one who attacked." Eithne said shocked.
"In the flesh. Yet you're the one at fault here."
Balaam responded.
"wh-What are you talking about?
You attacked us!"
Eithne scorned at the thought of her
being at fault for anything.
"I was the one who knew
of High-Mounts transgressions.
And what has your father, the King, done about it?
He and his prodigal court have squandered
the kingdom's resources elsewhere.
I had a solution yet I was mocked and outcasted!
Yet, I'm told of your proposals and solutions.
A perfect candidate for his plan.
Now, submit yourself to Aibphora,
so that High-Mount may find true
salvation which it has never found."
Balaam monologued all pompous.
"Or what? Don't you already
have your own kingdom!?"
Eithne scoffed in a defiant tone.
At this, Balaam's shadow emerged beside him
in the form of a blob made out of an unknown mass
armed with sharp angler-like teeth.

From there he covered Eithne's glass cage.
Pinning her where she stood, slowly covering
and absorbing her from the feet upward.
"You have two days to think this over.
Or become one with the one I serve."
He warned grimly.

I can't let him take me.
Who will rule the kingdom?
I am the queen to be!
I can't doom the kingdom!

Meanwhile, the young blacksmith was ready
for the journey that was ahead of him,
to depart on his noble and glorious quest to save his friend;
To save the princess from the clutches of the undead.
His mother had stopped him as he marched
towards the main gate of the kingdom.
"Aaron! Just what do you think you're doing?"
She inquired while very upset.
For Aaron did not tell his family. Oops.
"I'm gonna go and save her, Mom!"
Aaron proclaimed to his mom.
He then saw that she was in clear distress
and with that fear that all mothers have
when they see their sons go off to war.
"Mijo, this is suicide! Don't throw your
life away like this!" Aaron's mother pleaded.
"Mama... I have to do this, if it means saving

her and all of High-Mount, then I will!
Even if no one else will.
It's what you and Dad have taught me, right Mom?
To do what's right even if you're alone in doing it?
Well just you watch Mama,
I shall return with the princess and
there will be trumpets and dancing!"
Aaron explained so pompous yet assuring,
although he was not really sure of what
he was telling her would come true, even to himself.
His mother, while not agreeing with it,
knew he was right, though stubborn.
Just as she was. So, she concluded:
"Alright mijo. There is no persuading you out of it.
If you are this determined, them promise me this:
Both of you return alive."
They both embraced each other in a hug
as mother and son for what could be their last.

Remember them who gave you life!
Both your father and mother!
For in spite of the strife,
Without their teachings, why bother?

After their last hug before Aaron's quest,
She watched her youngest and only son
walk to the gates with a tear in her eye:
"May the Lord protect you and
bring you back home to me."

This was it, the gates out of the city.
"OPEN THE GATE!" yelled the guards.
The grand gate had lowered to the ground.
It was time for Aaron to take the first step.
Out to the fields of High-Mount
were the farmlands are.
His plan was through the forest,
towards the Mountain within.
Eithne for sure will be there!

The first steps to glory!
How grand it will be
to tell my story!
They for sure will agree!

Behind him the grand gates were closing,
he looked back towards his mother on the other side,
and gave her a modest and genuine smile,
as they waved to each other farewell.
Then those grand gates have closed...
No turning back now...good-bye Mom.
I hope to return alive, to you and Dad.
Aaron thought to himself.
Then he turned towards the barren farmlands.
They were dry and fruitless. Contaminated.
Though the greenery was alive, the food was not.
How tempting it was to stop and retreat.
Scary this quest will be, why go?
This thought tortured him to no end.

So, with sheathed Caelestis and shield in hand,
he thought it wise to make haste and ran.
He ran and he ran away from these thoughts.
He kept running and running through the fields.
Heatwaves were visible in the distance.
The whole area was covered in these
heatwaves which plagued the air with a metallic taste.
Filling Aaron's lungs with drops of blood
as he made haste to the forest.
Aaron could not give up, not when he started.
He saw the forest from afar, running towards it!
His gambeson and gear the heavier!
Nausea, then dizziness, upchucking.
Aaron was tiring by the minute,
but he remained resolute:

"Not today sloth!
I'm more diligent!
You are one I loath!
Your lotuses will not take me!"

He reached the forest that were often
preached against by the Court not to venture into.
"The Forest of Iniquity, I'm filled with pity for you."
Aaron uttered as he began to walk to it.
His breath slowly and steady,
being freshened with forest dew.
Aaron's pace leveled itself out.
Green and dark and crisp were the trees.

Yet the grass felt withered and crackly
like walking on broken glass as he further progressed.
Filled with mystery and emptiness
as if many sad memories resurfaced from childhood.
Many thought this was where
the ghouls and a variety of monsters ruled.
No one dared to enter,
for only a few have left these woods
the same as they entered.
I'll be the first to live, they'll see!
Aaron puffed to himself with a sense of pride.
Little did he know that he was being
watched the moment he entered.
"So the blacksmith really is a fool.
I'll send him another greeting party."
Aibphora said to himself.

"Woe to Icarus the fool!
The one who flew too high!
As Aaron more a fool!
The one who'll fall and die!"

After a time of walking and exploration,
it was time for rest.
Aaron looked and beheld in sheer surprise:
A pond with a small waterfall!
Though clean and clear was the pond water,
it flowed slowly and the waters were still.
To Aaron's surprise, there was greenery everywhere!

"I'll set up camp here." Aaron thought to himself.
A small campfire and food by the rim of the pond.
Though Aaron preferred to be in his warm bed,
he was on his own quest that's worth a thousand beds.
Drinking of the pond's freshwater,
he found that his energy had left him,
and so he rested his eyes for a while.

Rest, you who labor!
You who work in sunlight!
Night is the time to savor.
Then your soul shall be bright!

Little did he know he was being watched
by an unknown being who lives within these parts.
There was a hut just beyond the waterfall.
Who could live there? Why, it was someone.
That someone, was hidden within the waterfall,
she was just watching quietly, as if stalking prey.
Oh please, not another prize seeker after my head.
This someone readied, aimed, and fired from her bow
aiming for Aaron's shield to alarm him.
Aaron slept and he slept, then Splash!
He was awakened at the attack!
Drawing his Caelestis and shield on guard
then noticed the figure in the waterfall:
"W-Who goes there? Show yourself!"
"You'll desire my demise if I do!"
The figure warned in a slithery yet feminine voice.

"Do you... guard this pond by chance?"
Aaron asked genuinely but remaining on guard.
This question of course confused the figure.
So she emerged from the waterfall all wet.
"This is my home, so I do..." She answered.
Of course, to Aaron's surprise,
it was a serpentine woman!
She had a serpent tail rather than legs,
spanning what Aaron believed to be around
a total length of 35 feet long!
From the naval up was that of a woman,
but her head was still serpent-like.
Wearing rags for clothes with a bow and arrows.
Red hair like that of rubies and
snake-eyes like that of fiery ambers.
Her serpent pattern was that of a copperhead,
yet the colors of a milk-snake:
a pattern of red, black and white.
She was scary, and yet, to Aaron, was gorgeous.

What happened to her?
Was she always a snake?
Whose history is a blur.
All lives are at stake.

Feeling Aaron's presence to be a threat,
she drew another arrow and aimed.
"Explain yourself stranger!" she proclaimed.
Aaron not wanting a fight sheathed Caelestis.

Though he had his shield on standby.
"Listen, I'm just resting here for a while, ok?
For I am on a quest, to save the princess from
the Ghoul that's responsible for the famine
which plagues my kingdom!" Aaron said
being all pompous though a little uneasy.
This triggered a memory, a rather dark one.
Which made the serpentine lady question:
"You know of the Ghoul?"
"Yeah! He attacked my home,
and captured my friend,
so I'm gonna go and save her."
Aaron proclaimed all indignant.
"HA! Surely you jest." She prodded smugly.
"Don't push it amiga." Aaron warned,
annoyed at the jest of his recent blunder.
"You don't seem to be a warrior or a hunter."
Feeling he could trust her,
Aaron introduced himself:
"The truth is, you're right. I'm a blacksmith.
The name's Aaron. Aaron of High-Mount."
Surprised at this, she felt less irritated.
Now she was more intrigued, rather,
at the thought of not being hunted.
Although cautious, she slowly lowered her bow:
"Very well, you may have heard of me as
the Serpent of the Wood, but do know that
I am much more than that! My real name, is Elena."
Now, Aaron was eased at this introduction.

When two strangers meet,
Anything can happen.
When hearts be sweet,
A friendship can happen.

A familiar presence which, at sundown,
the twilight brought forth a cold and heavy air,
a familiar presence that Aaron felt.
The dread of that metallic taste in the air
and nausea began to plague his head once more.
Although it was nothing when compared to
Elena who senses were amplified by her curse.
From the woods came more undead, 40 in total.
"oh no... Get to cover, quick!" Aaron ordered.
"No, this is my home and I'm defending it!"
Seeing her determination, he was moved.
He drew out Caelestis again and Elena her bow!
"Alright, we'll take them on together!"
The screams of the undead shrieked as they charged,
many of them ran as a group as a few were scattered.
Some were slow, while others sprinted.
Aaron charged at one as he bashed his shield into
one's skull and slashed down the torso of another undead.
Elena coiled as a snake does when defending.
Then drew arrow after arrow,
headshot after headshot,
not a single one could get near to her.
Until one dodged a shot, pounced towards her.

Aaron saw this and charged, pounced towards
the living nightmare with Caelestis to save Elena.
Then SLASH! Head rolling and body lifeless.

Could this be?
A Human...saved, me?
He wants me to live?
What does he want with me?

Slashes and swishes and arrows and strikes.
SLASH! WHOOSH! BASH! PIERCE!
They fought valiantly until all the undead fell.
Until those screams of the damned were silenced.
Aaron was tired and out of breath: "You... alright?"
"Yes, my home, protected." Elena responded while
out of breath while still on guard for any opponents.
"Surely, that was amazing!" Aaron was impressed.
Elena was not sure how to react to this:
"I just did it to protect my home."
Since Aaron did not want any trouble
with this scary yet gorgeous snake woman,
he wanted to leave on good terms with her.
So he says triumphantly:
"Now you see what I have to fight against ahead.
Thanks for your help and I hope you live a good life.
If it's the same with you, I'll be on my way."

A man with valor.
A monster with a soul.

Both against the hoard.
Until they return to Sheol.

I don't get it. He's not after me or my head.
Why did he help me? Does he speak the truth?
Only one way to find out.
She thought to herself, then stopped Aaron:
"Hold it! It would be suicide if you fight them alone!
I may not care about your kingdom,
but IF it means I could live in peace,
then I want in. So, I'm coming with."
Aaron, not wanting any trouble,
thought it would be good to have
her company and assistance.
Although He still hopes not to be
killed or eaten in his sleep.
"Very well, we can share in the glory!"
He replied as he cleared his throat.
And so after a night's rest and recovery,
Aaron set on his quest to save Eithne.
This time, with a new companion.

The human and she-snake.
A friendship with lore.
The undead shall shake.
For both souls are evermore.

The blacksmith and the monster, now a duo.
Two with differing goals, yet a common cause.

Walking and always on guard for anymore undead.
After a while, they found something unusual.
Lying on a tree was a rusting figure.
It appeared to be a man of bronze and iron:
At 7 feet tall, a knight helmet for a head.
A bronze body covered in armor with iron limbs.
From pauldrons and gauntlets to
grieves and sabatons and an armored kilt.
It seems it had a crossbow with advanced features.
This fascinated Aaron since he, as a blacksmith,
always liked learning about how everything works:
"Wait a minute, I've heard tales about this as a child.
How is this real? Wait... who made it?"
"Don't! I don't want to have to fight
this thing if it were to lives again.
Someone must've left it here for a reason."
Elena said, recognizing the metal creature during
a time of exploring the forest long ago.
"You know of this thing?" Aaron asked, surprised.
"Yeah, it was something I found long ago,
but I would rather just leave it be."
She explained as if it were a bad memory.

Memories of Bronze.
Rather bitter and cold.
Fighting against Brawns,
can be made into gold.

"What happened exactly?" Aaron wondered.

"Let's just say there's... history." Elena evaded.

Aaron wanted to bring it back to life,

but knew it unsettles Elena. So he decided:

"...Maybe so, but maybe, just maybe,

we could persuade it somehow.

If it fights us, then we fight."

"...Fine." Elena said begrudgingly.

Aaron then took a closer inspection at the metal man

and discovered the inner workings were unknown.

The sweat, the blisters, and all the metal parts

and fluids were gnawing away at his patience.

"Trabaja pedazo de caca!"

Aaron yelled being very hot-tempered.

Then he discovered a few disconnections

and a couple of what seemed to be a few switches.

With a hammer and bandages, there were blue eyes.

"...lllllllll...Life...Reanimated..."

The metal figure spoke with a metallic

yet rough and damaged voice.

Elena was on her guard against a figure of her past.

Whereas Aaron was startled that he actually fixed it:

"Huh. Didn't think that would work!"

The figure saw both of them

and had no memory of anything,

their arms transformed into a crossbow in one arm,

and a weird mechanism which could breathe fire in the other.

Aaron suspected it to be a Greek Fire.

This Goliath of a bronze Golem exclaimed:

"Unknown persons detected. Identify yourselves!"

Aaron held his shield and Elena with her bow ready.

"Who are these individuals?
Priorities in order for fulfillment.
Priorities are not these individuals.
Perhaps they may assist in fulfillment."

"Hold on a minute amigo! I am Aaron of High-Mount!"
He yelled still with shield in hand.
"Processing...Identity accepted."
The figure said as their mechanical brain processed.
It then turned to Elena: "Identify yourself!"
"..." Elena was still coiled on guard.
Unsure to reveal herself to the metal creature.
"Identity invalid, identify yourself!"
The figure demanded, determined to know.
"Alright fine! I am Elena!" Elena exclaimed.
"Identity accepted! You are not priority. Priority remains."
The figure stated in his rough voice.
"Wait, wait, wait, slow down now!"
Aaron said intervening between them.
After all three slowed and de-escalated themselves,
all three of them gave account of who they were.
"Alright, I'm on a quest to save High-Mount's Princess,
and I may need help. If we win, we can share in glory."
Aaron explained hoping not to cause a conflict.
"I'm just helping if it means
not being hunted anymore."
Elena stoically explained hoping not

to set off the metal man into a frenzy.

"Priorities remain:

-      regain memory

-      smite down traitor.

Error, who is this traitor?"

The figure wondered.

"Well it's settled then; we help each other then."

Look at these three misfits!
An unexpected alliance.
Let's call them the Heroic Misfits!
In each other will be reliance.

"Wait a minute. How will this thing not betray us?"

Elena asked skeptically.

"Identity: Eidolon, servant of [Redacted].

Alliances:

-      Aaron of High-Mount,

-      Elena, Serpentine Lady."

Eidolon said in their metallic voice.

"I guess that's our answer?" Aaron questioned unsure.

"Another thing, it's Elena. Not 'sErPeNtInE lAdY'"

She said annoyed as anyone would being mocked.

"Alliances: Aaron of High-Mount, and Elena."

Eidolon corrected being indifferent of course.

"Alright then.

The blacksmith, serpentine, and metal creature.

No one will mess with us!"

Aaron puffed, annoyingly optimistic.

So the Heroic Misfits had made their alliance.
On a quest to save Princess Eithne and to stop
Balaam and that demonic-being he was with.

Problem resolved between them?
Though not a perfect group,
they are like shiny gems.
An unorthodox troupe.

3

THE HELLISH NIGHTMARE

Upon awakening,
Eithne saw that she was consumed
from the naval down within the demonic sludge.
She struggled and struggled but to no avail.
Oh Aaron, wherever you are, please hurry.
Of course, this caught Balaam's attention
and so began to interrogate her again.
"Why must you persist Princess?
You can save yourself by serving Aibphora.
And yet, your blacksmith has found us."
So he has come for me? Eithne thought.
"It's a shame that he's returned for his death.
I will show him and his companions a little greeting."
Balaam responded smugly.
With this, Balaam's shadow left him
to reach the entrance to the place.

The guests of honor are here.
Them to enter hell's gate.

What's ahead they should fear.
And Eithne's the bait!

The stench of the undead had
plagued the air with its presence.
The heat of an invisible force surrounded it.
Our Heroic Misfits had no other choice
but to suffered through the heavy heat.
Even though it made Aaron and Elena
a little woozy and dizzy as they pushed through,
then the truth was revealed on what they saw.
What's this, not a mountain, but a citadel!
Why, this was the Eckhert Citadel!
It was clothed in dark obsidian with that same
mild orange hue that surrounded the undead.
The sheer sight was that of Brackenridge Palace!
Yet, the Eckhert Citadel had more towers and was
taller in comparison to Brackenridge Palace.
Its foundation was that of a circular Ziggurat
with a diameter of 273 acres.
With one grand yet zigzagged staircase
which led to the Citadel itself.
It was crowned with a palace on top.
Robed with grand walls and sturdy towers
that was ready to endure any battle it faced.
And yet, it looked from the outside that it
could have been its own city-state as well.
"So, this is it. Honestly, I thought it was a mountain."
Elena commented while seeing Aaron in awe.

"It reminds me of home, yet... that of a dark reflection."
Aaron said as if trying to see past a pareidolia.
"I knew it was a palace, I could just sense it."
Elena responded, smelling with her forked tongue.
"Memory error. Priorities remains the same."
Eidolon responded while also starring at it alongside Aaron,
although he was analyzing it rather than in awe.
"May the LORD protect us," Aaron prayed quietly.

Into the darkness of nightmares,
Our heroes dare enter Hades.
They proceed with care,
Against dead brigades.

Brittle and long was the bridge.
Extended for over half a mile long.
No one was on guard.
For the living enter, into the dead.
Who could ever enter and live?
Our three misfits proceeded carefully.
Walking and sticking to the center when they could.
Crackle, crumble, tumble went the stairs.
As is slowly crumbled at the weight of these misfits.
Elena had to slither slowly, very slowly.
Aaron tip-toed upon the brittle stones.
Tap, leap, tap, leap, tap, light on his toes.
Eidolon had to run once they made it safely across.
Portions slowly falling and collapsing.
Though slow, the grand stairs

began to collapse behind them.
Then crack, crud, crack, crud went the bridge!
Everyone is now running for their lives!
Surely, they will die if they lose ground
at the height they were at!
Running for their lives to the gate!
Elena and Eidolon had made it,
only for Aaron to do the leap of faith!

Tread carefully you reckless!
Slow down, you impatient!
For life is not a guess!
Wise you who are patient.

"Rope would have sufficed." Eidolon patronized.
"There was no other way! I don't even have any!"
Aaron responded, all stressed and irritated.
"Does it matter now? We lived and crossed!"
Elena huffed, annoyed of the bickering.
"Ok fine, fine, we made it.
Alive, not dead. Perfect,"
Aaron went on irritated,
"Besides, there's no turning back now."
"Priority set:
-     Re-obtain lost memories
-     terminate traitor and sludge
-     Save Princess of High-Mount."
Eidolon stated, determined to fulfill these priorities.
Upon climbing the grand stairs,

there an ominous gate coated in obsidian
and faintly glowing orange hues.
Dark and grand it was, within the gate,
a side door of the same look.
Eidolon broke it down with their brute strength.
Clash! Bang! Crash!
Upon entering through these gates
was a main plaza that was found in ruins.
"I dare to hope that the princess is here.
I wish not for her demise or for my humiliation."
Aaron responded both concerned and determined.

No king dared have their knights sent,
For Sin and Death dwell in these halls.
Into the darkness our heroes went
With all the writings on the walls...

They all investigated the plaza and saw it overrun
with overgrowth and those same blobs Aaron
saw throughout the fields of High-Mount.
This time upon the grand stairs.
Its aura with its horrible vibe,
the emission was everywhere again.
Creaky and kooky and spooky everywhere.
"Please keep away from those blobs."
Aaron warned, being sure to keep away himself.
"Affirmative." Eidolon responded.
"Yep, your princess definitely is here then."
Elena responded in a sarcastic yet playful way.

Where the grand doors of one building
across from the main gate opened,
in it, there was a void within those doors.
Humming and whooshing and growling.
Shadowy hands had grabbed the three, to consume.
Elena had grabbed the railings with her serpentine tail,
holding onto Aaron for dear life!
Eidolon holding onto Aaron!
"Hold on!" She yelled in pain.
"WHY WOULD I DARE NOT TO!?" Aaron shouted.
More and more shadowy hands extended
from the void destroying the railing,
consuming the three misfits.
Then silence! In the darkness they lay.
"Ugg, my hea-wait... Eidolon? Elena!?"
Aaron exclaimed all alone, in the darkness.

Woe unto the one with pride!
For isolation is their end!
From people they hide!
For darkness is their end!

From his pack was a lantern, but it was destroyed.
Then from behind, the recurring humming noise.
"A mere light will not help you."
A voice reached out.
"Huh? Who's there... show yourself!"
Aaron yelled into the darkness of the room.
Then there was more silence within the darkness.

A wind blew through the room, orange lights lit.
The room ran rampant with the obsidian and coldness.
Aaron then drew Caelestis in one hand
and his shield in the other.
Ready to fight whoever lurked within the dark.
"Why should I? I'm everywhere.
In the light, and in the shadows, all around you,
and within you..." Riddled the droning voice.
"What are you talking about?" Aaron asked.

I dwell in the darkness
Within the human heart.
The world is a mess,
Thus sin is my art.

Then from the walls oozed that nauseating sludge,
Slowly, crawling, the hues glowed bright and dim
as if it were breathing. Forming into a human.
"Agh!" Aaron jumped back, startled.
"Oh no need to be alarmed,
for I am merely a part of you,"
assured the sludge figure.
"You're not making any sense,"
Aaron responded confused.
"No need to, just embrace it.
For I am you, I am known too only a few.
Aibphora is the name." they said.
"I-I don't think I'm part-sludge."
Aaron said timid yet humorous.

"QUIET you imbecile!" Aibphora shouted angrily.
Aaron was startled at the boom.
Prompting Aaron to yell defensively:
"No need to be angry over something silly!"
"But is this not how you're treated, blacksmith?
A laughingstock to the Kingdom?" Aibphora responded.

A fool is the ego!
Inflated with hubris.
Where did the glory go?
Into the abyss.

Aaron knew deep down Aibphora was right,
the words swelled up with the bitterness
of those disgusting blobs,
"I was mocked and laughed at.
I know this to be true."
Aibphora could sense it,
a crack in the young man's character.
His Achilles Heel so to speak,
and seized after it as a predator with its' prey.
"Do not feel bad, for God has designed the world
in this unfair way. The righteous get poorer,
while the wicked get richer and richer."
Aibphora claimed in an argumentized manner.
"No He didn't. For He is fair and just.
In fact, I should know." Aaron responded.
"Say that to those suffering of pestilence and war!
To those subject to tyranny and servitude!

No matter how much you long for peace,
you never receive it!
You're nothing but a servant to gluttons,
young blacksmith! Don't you see!?"
The bitter and metallic words once again
wrapped around Aaron's heart.
Clenched it as if a heavy burden sunk it.
But Aaron felt bolder still,
bold enough to respond:
"Even if this were true,
it's people who are guilty of such things,
not the LORD my God.
I know He is who he claims to be!
I witnessed His mercy and compassion.
He shows it to all!"
Such a response filled Aibphora's whole being
with such malice that he snapped:
"MERCY!? HAhahahaha! Such foolery!
God designed the world so the innocent
Will pay for the sins of those in power.
Those GLUTTONS AND MADMEN!...
Oh... you know about this already?
The young man who just wants to be good
and to belong. Yet was repaid with hatred
and ostracization by those around him.
IS THAT FAIR!? IS THIS WHAT YOU WANT!?"
Aaron could feel the discouragement and agony.
Needles piercing his brain and his heart.
Nausea and a pit took hold. Again.

Oh such hatred!
Who can stand it?
All there be, is red!
No one can admit.

"You know for yourself
that you were born for glory,
and not born for destitution.
However, there is a solution..."
With the wave of his hand,
Aibphora summoned into the hall:
A unique suit of armor.
Equipped with a Zwei-hander.
This armor looked to be of a dark metal
with that same orange hue like the rest of the place.
Complete with a helmet, breastplate, backplate,
pauldrons, gauntlets, grieves, and sabatons,
the soft padding clothes beneath this suit of armor
did not look like a traditional gambeson.
Rather, it looked like some second skin which
connected the armor pieces to each other.
As for the Zwei-hander,
it seemed to have also been made
from a dark metal which emitted
some kind of energy once one was near it,
emitting that same nauseating
orange hue oozed from it!
Yet, it appealing to Aaron, his ego intrigued.

Captivating at the sight of the ominous yet epic armor set.
He could not help but feel entranced.
"W-Wow. That looks incredible." He said with glee.
As Aaron walked up to it,
he began to feel a sensation
that could only be fuzziness and tingling.
Little did he know of what was really happening.

You foolish Blacksmith!
Do you not know right from wrong?
Death stares at you with a scythe!
Your life towards a swift end...

"This is yours; you can set things right!
To do what your God failed to do!"
The offer vibes with the blend of
metal and grease within a sense of fuzziness.
He wanted the glory he thought was due for himself.
All that power, all that glory and fortune!
At last, he could be on high and not be lowly!
The thought of it filled his veins with vigor!
Then... from the deepest depths of his heart,
perhaps from the deepest depths of his brain,
Aaron couldn't explain it, but he could sense it.
A quiet and gentle voice, it pleaded with him,
bringing to memory Christ's goodness.
All this was worth living for to him.
His family and friends. If he took this offer,
what would happen to him?

What would this armor do to him?
This fuzziness, why is it stinging a little?
He could not betray them like this!
He could not ignore the blasphemy
spoken by the fiend floating before him.
Moved from glee to sorrow, this be Aaron's answer:
"Your offer appeals to me, but at what cost?
To betray the LORD my God?
The one who I love and has loved me?
Though I am great and gorgeous,
my soul and eternity shall not be sold!"

Blessed are the Martyrs,
for their souls are pure.
This world has no barter,
For Christ is the cure!

At this proclamation,
Aibphora quizzed angrily:
"You forgive God this folly?
For making you a servant and not a hero!?
You were made for glory! To have everything!"
This moved Aaron to respond in humility:
"The truth is, I may be great,
I want this fortune and glory,
but I'm not gonna do it like this!
Truly, I am a blacksmith,
but God had done everything for me!
He gave me a home, an amazing family!

Now he's called me for a time like this.
To stop you and your servant!
My friends, I shall rescue!
And if I die trying, so be it!"
With boldness in his heart,
he stood ready to fight!

Humility is true beauty!
It restores the soul!
Convicted by duty,
It makes one whole!

At this, Aibphora drew bear-like claws,
an orange aura was stirring from him
"So be it, you fool..."
Aaron was to use Caelestis,
yet Aibphora slapped it away!
Now his last defense, his shield!
SLASH! BASH! CLASH!
Went Aibphora's claws at Aaron.
A metallic taste plagued Aaron's mouth
then came the nausea and fatigue once again.
All Aaron could do was to hold his shield.
With both hands holding on for dear life!
Hiding behind it as if he were a turtle!
SLASH! BASH! CLASH!
Both had tired after two minutes,
Smiting and defending with all their might!

The taste of metal.
Nausea and fatigue.
Its effects brutal.
Worse than a plague.

At his final strike, Aibphora roared panting,
"ARGH! Smiting you down will be a waste!
But mark my words blacksmith,
when the time is right,
you and those you love shall fall at my hand!"
At this, Aibphora had vanished.
This allowed Aaron to take a moment's rest.
Though collapsing to his knees in exhaustion.
Panting, shaking, though hopeful.
He regained his footing,
and resolved to find the exit and his friends.
he then gave praise the LORD:

Blessed be Christ!
My hope and redeemer!
I was tempted with vice,
Yet He has delivered me!

4

THE SHIVERING SERPENT

"**Impossible! I had him in my claws!**
The Armor was his to take,
and he was mine to steal,
mine to kill and destroy!
No matter, his doom and yours will be soon."
Aibphora said to Eithne aggravated.
At this point the sludge consumed Eithne
from the bust down to the floor
inside of her glass blown cage.
"I-I knew that Aaron would win..."
Eithne said smugly yet weakly.
As the demonic sludge slowly consumes her heart,
but not entirely, yet, for there was still time left
before she would be fully consumption.
But this will not stop her from
holding out for her dear friend.
Aibphora and Balaam starred in surprise
as they miscalculated how willful the Princess is.
"Ugh, your arrogance will be your end, Princess.

What we have in store, all shall meet their end."
Balaam scorned while staring in annoyance.
At this, he turned with a swagger,
whooshing his cape,
leaving the throne room.

Confidence or arrogance,
either way, the Princess resolved.
To her, Aaron is no dunce.
His faith and heart also resolved.

Meanwhile, Elena found herself in a new section of
Eckhert Citadel where the room was circular
in shape and was all wet and cool.
All she could remember was holding onto
Aaron and then there was pure darkness.
"A-Aaron? Eidolon? Where'd they go?"
Elena wondered; calm yet concerned.
The cool atmosphere was now starting to bite
every inch of the room from top to bottom.
An old familiar atmosphere,
buried within a memory.
With bow and arrow armed,
however, Elena was cold-blooded,
and her blood was slowing down, freezing.
Why, her very blood was that of ice!
This atmosphere was worse than before,
something freezing, icing, paralyzing...
Squirming for her life, she could not speak.

Shivering, freezing, dying!
What is this? What's in the air, WHAT IS THIS!!
Elena thought to herself while in agony.
Even though she thought she was dying,
something was keeping her alive.

How cold is the isolation
That I shiver in agony?
Why am I desolate?
To be forever lonely...

Then there was *him.*
A figure unfamiliar to her.
Yet, a forgotten memory?
"How life has treated you so poorly, dear Elena."
The figure told her gravely and roughly.
She could not speak but could only look up.
Painfully, shakily. Confused by the voice.
"You don't remember, do you?"
The figure asked as they slowly lit torches
with a wave of his halberd.
Flickers, pops, snickers.
Each torch ignited sparked a memory,
the horrors, all coming back!
The cold air surrounded her body, petrifying.
It was HIM, the adversary which Aaron
has sought to find and slay to rescue his friend.
Wait... no... it can't be!
The nightmares... Mom, Dad...

Elena thought to herself as Balaam's
eye brought back that time long ago.

Trapped in the Abyss
This poor Medusa.
Despair within darkness
will hope dare thaw?

With the torches lit,
Elena was still pinned,
but could finally speak.
"Y-you... it can't be..."
She uttered coldly with grief and horror.
"You lived, after all of these years.
And now, all alone once again."
He boasted sinisterly and snickering.
"W-where are they," She demanded.
"...Even now, your companions suffer your fate.
To die in agony and despair.
Pawns in a great game."
Balaam proclaimed gravely and full of himself.
Elena's thoughts ran through her mind:

This can't be the end!
Was my life for nothing?
I must fulfill my amend!
This can't be the ending!

Balaam approached the shivering serpentine,

and grabbed her by her leathery throat
to hold her shake her around like a ragdoll.
"I should've slaughtered you
like the monster you were born to be."
Balaam said with great malice.
He then slams her to the floor,
holding her head to it with his gloved hand.
"Unless... having you here to rot should suffice.
If you must know, you shall learn your family's fate."
Balaam said, looking down upon the poor girl.
"W-what?" Elena asked coldly.
"Yesss." Balaam hissed mockingly.
"It was I that made you this way.
Your family revealed my plans
before High-Mount's Royal Court.
It was because of this,
I was exiled because of those bootlickers
that your parents and all the kingdom were.
So I found my revenge upon them.
Cursing them by cursing you.
With you here, dying at my hand.
What I failed to do that day,
my revenge is now complete.
You and that blacksmith.
All shall meet the fates you deserve."

Woe to those who seek revenge!
For you are never satisfied.
When you do avenge,

empty is your heart inside.

Upon these words,
Balaam had vanished from Elena.
Leaving her for her inevitable doom.
The room continued to grow cold and dark.
Elena's blood, frozen and shivering.
Her condition worsening minute by minute.
This only left her bleak and defeated.
So he is the one to blame for my misery!
He is to blame for my family's demise!
They were everything to me!
AAAAAAAAAAAAAARGH!!!
The air was now at sub-zero levels.
Frostbite and pale was she.
Aaron... Eidolon... I... I can't...
let them... die... They need me... I... will...
At this final thought,
she succumbed to the bitter freezing darkness.
Yet, she resolved in her heart:
Even if she was to die here,
she was no longer alone in this world.
She has people to care about again,
Aaron and Eidolon.
Yet, where are they?

Be encouraged!
You who are lonely,
For your dread

is temporary only.

After who knows how long has passed,
The atmosphere was warm yet sterile.
She saw what seemed abstract.
A dream-like space with colors upward.
Yet, in every other direction was a white limbo.
This could not be Heaven nor Hell.
This can't be Purgatory either.
Wherever it was, it was of spiritual origin.
Where am I? Am I...dead? She thought.
She looked down to see herself,
and what did she see?
Not red scales and claws,
but olive skin and nails!
Where her fangs were, human teeth!
Her hair was the same, yet a brunette!
And her eyes!
Not serpentine, but human!
Elena was human!
For the first time!
What is this place?

How can this be?
Flesh and not scales?
Am I truly free?
No more serpent tails!

The confusion then turned into horror as she

noticed a void in the distance.
The same void that dragged the three misfits.
Elena tried to draw her bow,
but to her shock, it was gone.
So she then held up her fist, struggling to stand.
She wobbled and struggled.
No matter the effort, she could not walk.
She gave all she got to crawl for her life.
Then eventually could no longer crawl!
She had no choice but to face the void.
With courage in her heart, she faced it.
As the void was about to consume her,
The colors above beamed a fiery light upon it!
Weakening the void to mere nothingness.
Sizzle! Sizzle! Fizzle...
The colors, all angelic-like, exclaimed:

"Do not be afraid!
The LORD is with you!
Your friends are at your aid!
These words be true!"

Then, it faded to silence and black.
Though she was faint,
A certain presence arrived.
Overtime, she felt her body slowly
but surely start to warm up.
Something was covering her, protecting her.
Something warm, soft, cloth-like.

A comfort long forgotten now found.
Then was a familiar voice,
not a malicious one,
but rather one she knew of, was fond of:
"...elena... Elena... Elena?"
She slowly opened her eyes,
disoriented and regaining.
Once recomposed, there they were.
Aaron and Eidolon by her side.
She found herself wrapped up in Aaron's cloak.
They were in a warm and cozy place
somewhere within Eckhert Citadel.
A saferoom, so to speak.
Why, it looked like an old bedroom.
"Elena, are you alright?" Aaron asked all angsty.
"Aaron. i-is it you?" Elena asked softly.
"Yes, it is! I thought you were dead!" Aaron replied.
"Priority fulfilled: Find companions," Eidolon stated.
She then embraced Aaron (which he accepted).
"Please, let's not be separated again,"
Aaron asked in a joking manner as he thought
it would help boost morale between the three,
but made it just a little awkward for everyone.
"Agreed. But your cloak is mine now."
Elena responded wrapping herself up
with its warm and well-tailored wool.
"Priority set:
-      Re-obtain lost memories
-      terminate traitor and sludge

-       Save Princess of High-Mount"
Eidolon stated with a mechanical nod.
"Let us finish this and save the Princess."
Aaron concluded to both of his companions.
With this and Elena's recovery,
they set forth to the tallest tower.

How sweet is a reunion!
Friends found once more.
Strong is their communion.
Down to the very core.

5

THE LIVING METAL

Upon his return, Balaam learned that Elena
had survived the shivering encounter:
"WHAT'S THIS!? She was dead, I ensured it!"
Enraged, he struck the floor with a giant's stomp!
He turned towards Eithne
who was now consumed from the neck down
by the demonic sludge and said to her:
"I'm afraid you were right to place
your faith in your heroic fraud.
It's a shame that it's all for nothing."
"I-If I am to die, I shall not convert to your
pointless crusade against my kingdom!"
Eithne proclaimed with all she had left in her.
With the impact of a scorched frying pan,
Balaam scornfully slapped Eithne with his backhand
as a rebuke for her simple act of fortitude:
"Even as you conform to be Aibphora's servant,
you remain resolute in your folly!?
Your will and your hope are misplaced Eithne!

Soon, Aibphora shall consume you as he did me!
Only then will you become High-Mount's Queen
as you were meant to be!"

Near her very end,
She will be consumed.
If no one will amend,
The Princess is doomed.

Meanwhile, all that Eidolon could process
was holding onto a railing
and then came the swift silence.
Upon rebooting, Eidolon emphasized to himself:
"Companions missing,
Priority set:
-      Re-obtain lost memories
-      terminate traitor and sludge.
-      Save Princess of High-Mount."
Purpose: unknown. Why?
What am I? Who is my maker?
Once mission is complete, what will I be?
Eidolon was on the search as he
'thought' upon these things.
his surroundings showed a dark room,
like that of obsidian and the orange hue.
Then, Aibphora the sludge demon appeared.
As before, he had his angler-like mouth.
"Hostile detected! Identify yourself!"
Eidolon screeched with authority.

**"I am merely what lies within the hearts of all.
And yet, you don't have one. Why is that?
What are you made for, knight of metal?"**
Aibphora said as per usual, introducing himself.
"Name and/or title not recognized,"
Eidolon replied.

*A mechanical heart.
Filled with purpose.
Is this true art?
Who would ever know?*

Eidolon equipped himself with his crossbow arm:
"Origin: Unknown. Termination in progress!"
Even though Aibphora saw an asset,
Eidolon could not be moved by his tricks or deals.
"So be it, Golem." Aibphora said with claws equipped.
Eidolon had made the first move.
Ready, aim, and release they went,
arrows flying, direct hit!
Only to no avail were said arrows.
Against a thick and fluid creature.
It was of no use against such demon.
**"You fool, your conventional weaponry
are useless against me!
All who strike me shall despair.
And you won't stop, will you?
Have at you then!"**
Aibphora yelled, amused by his ego.

Arrows flew and claws slashed as they
fought and dodged each attack!
Eidolon, heavy on his feet stood firm as a sentry.
Aibphora swift in the air dodging each arrow.
Even though they are useless.
After a minute, one arrow had landed!
Though to Aibphora's surprise,
it pinned him in place as said arrow began to burn.

How foolish is sin!
Puffed with hubris!
With the weed within,
will end rootless!

For over another minute had gone by,
Eidolon continued arrow after arrow.
Shot after shot, Aibphora was worn but not out.
Heavy and gravel breaths were the sludge demon's:
"I seem to have under-estimated you,
brave knight of metal.
Such power could conquer many great nations!"
Aibphora exclaimed sinisterly yet very winded.
Eidolon then switched out his crossbow,
only for the right hand to transform into
a mechanism which breathed fire and smoke.
"Arrows deemed useless; flames activated."
He pointed it towards Aibphora.
A small light began to grow within his arm device.
Then Aibphora was blasted away by

a massive napalm engulfing the room!
Then followed yells and screams of agony!
Weakening that Eldridge sludge.
Now melted and slithered away to safety.
Leaving puddles and blobs like the ones found
in the plaza upon entering
a dreadful place like this!
"You have bested me for now,
but mark my words, knight of metal,
your might and will shall fail you."
Eidolon, believing the fight has been won,
had proclaimed to himself:
"Priority complete. Previous priorities in order:
Find companions. Rescue Princess of High-Mount."
With this, Eidolon found the door to escape.

In flames went the sludge!
The sinful sludge from hell!
For it will face the Judge
and return where they fell!

Eidolon bashed through the door.
Shards and planks went flying,
he found a torch and lit it with their hand.
Back into the dark he went to fulfill his set priorities.
I have arms with weapons, what are they for?
Was I made a knight?
Was I made for destruction?
What am I once all is destroyed?

Further analysis is required.
Eidolon continued to process these questions
for what seemed to him like an hour,
What was now right-side up is now topsy-turvy.
Up was down and down was up,
right was left and left was right.
Eidolon heard a distant and familiar voice:
"...Elena? ...Eidolon?"
"Companion voice detected,"
Eidolon said to himself.
They followed the voice, louder and louder
did the voice and footsteps approach,
"Wait, those steps... Eidolon?" The voice wondered.
Then, around the corner was Aaron!
"Eidolon!" He yelled as he approached him.
"Companion found.
Priority set:
- Re-obtain lost memories
- terminate traitor and sludge
- Save Princess of High-Mount."
Eidolon said to Aaron.
The two of them stuck close.
As they ventured deeper into the Eckhert Citadel.

Amid darkness,
There is always a light.
A friend will God bless,
where a sufferer will delight.

Colder and darker did this duo venture.

Once more, what was right-side up is topsy-turvy.

Up was down and down was up,

right was left and left was right.

Then they found a door, a dark blue door.

It was cold to the touch,

and locked was the door shut.

From within, they heard shivering and a faint voice.

"Companion voice detected!" Eidolon alerted.

"ELENA!" Aaron yelled in shock.

Aaron pulled off his backpack,

then drew out a hammer and pick.

CLINK! CLANK! BANG!

His hammer went at the door, but to no avail.

"Eidolon, can you thaw it?" Aaron asked.

Eidolon transformed his hand and started to glow.

Aaron stepped out of the way.

Eidolon then proceeded to incinerate

the door to mere ashes.

They looked and beheld their companion,

their friend, on the verge of death.

They both scooped Elena up into their arms

to deliver her to safety.

It was a struggle for the both of them

to drag their 35 footlong friend.

However, they managed to find a saferoom

free of any hostile influence.

A trio of friends,

Faced with death.
Will be there to the end,
To their last breath.

Though she be faint,
her heart was beating slowly.
Aaron drew his cloak and blanketed her in it.
"Elena?... Elena!" Aaron said in angst.
"Companion needs rest." Eidolon told Aaron.
Though she rested, Aaron never left her side.
She slowly opened her eyes,
Aaron and Eidolon by her side.
"Elena, are you alright?"
Aaron asked with angst.
 "...Aaron." Elena said softly.
She then embraced him with a hug
(which he did not expect).
Eidolon felt something at the sight of them.
Something from within, something...alive?
A flame? A core? ...A soul?
Why do I help them?
I have no need to help them.
Why do I? Why do I?
Why do I? Why do I?
Do they give me purpose?
Why do I-do I-I.
Analysis required.
"Anyway, what happened to you?" Aaron asked.
"...The adversary you seek is here.

He's most definitely here." Elena responded.

 "Really? I also faced him too. It was...awful..."

Aaron said hesitantly,

since he hated the experience.

So he continued to say:

"I know now what we face,

and I cannot face him alone.

Are you both still with me?"

Eidolon continued to process all that had happened.

Analysis complete. Priority absolved:

-   Re-obtain lost memories

Aaron and Elena resurrected me.

They did not have to.

However, assisting them has given me purpose

I will return their charity."

He fully processed this deep within his metal brain

and his mechanical heart, so he stated to them both:

"Priority set:

-    Terminate Aibphora.

-    Rescue Princess of High-Mount."

"I'm with you, to the end." Elena resolved.

With this resolution, they rested,

then set forth to the tallest tower.

How sweet a reunion!

Friends found once more.

Strong is their communion.

Down to the very core.

6

— · —

THE FLOATING CITADEL

After a few hours have past
since the Heroic Misfits
had entered Eckhert Citadel,
Princess Eithne's outlook did not look so good.
For her entire body except for her face was
now consumed by the demonic sludge.
Just a minute away from full consumption.
Aaron, I held out as long as I could...
may we meet again in a better life...
Eithne thought as her mind went.
"Times up Princess. What will it be?"
Balaam pressed as Eithne was only seconds away
from her demonic consumption.
"I'll... still... be queen... regardless..."
Eithne answered while gasping for air as
The sludge creeped its way into her mouth.
Balaam staring with scorn:
"Pity. You'll still belong to him either way."
At this, it was now too late for the Princess,

What was once life, now a statue.
Petrified as if she died screaming.

The Princess has fallen.
Our heroes were too late.
Oh how Eithne has fallen!
Why have this tragic fate?

As the Heroic Misfits made their way through
the abyss to the tower's top,
from up to down and down to up.
From left to right and right to left.
After a while, they lost track of
where they were until they found an obsidian stairwell,
with the only way they thought was up.
"I believe this is it.
There's no turning back once we ascend."
Aaron warned knowing what could be ahead.
"Once again. Like I told you, I am with you to the end."
Elena answered softly yet confident.
"Priority set:
-    Terminate Aibphora.
-    Rescue Princess of High-Mount."
Eidolon said, determined with crossbow arm equipped.
"Very well, let's go amigos!" Aaron said with zeal.

Up went the Heroes
to ascend the stairs.
These misfit zeroes,

with no more despair.

Up and up they went,
or what they thought was up.
They found themselves at a gate
with spirals and halberds decorating it,
like that which consumed them earlier.
Eidolon melted the lock, and with all their might,
they gave a giant smite to the door!
Within the tallest tower was a grand throne room,
though it was all dark and cold,
there was a golden throne on the other side,
Stained-glass windows with a mix of
purples, oranges, and greys.
Portraying a history all too familiar to Aaron.

Is this in Hell?
The traitor's fate?
No, just a shell,
of High-Mount's state...

Upon the Throne was him.
The cloaked figure from before.
The one who took Eithne,
The one who cursed her.
The one named Balaam.
"I seem to have underestimated you.
You and your two companions."
Balaam remarked smugly.

"Where is she?" Aaron asked, annoyed.
With one hand, he pointed up.
Above the throne,
to Aaron's horror,
was Princess Eithne, petrified.
Fully consumed by the sludge,
terrified, reaching out for help,
like a trophy to be displayed
before High-Mount's enemies.
The Heroic Misfits were too late.
"no..." Aaron muttered upset
beneath his breath and his helmet.

There she was
his best friend.
In a pause,
near her very end.

Balaam had stood up from the throne,
feeling he had won, proclaimed this monologue
with all his inflated hubris and ego:
"She did put up a good fight,
and yet I reign victorious.
Now, she serves as the first of a new era.
You may think of me as evil,
but this was needed for High-Mount's good.
The royalty has failed to help their own people.
Those I swore to protect.
Consumed by their wealth and jewels.

Fat from their gluttony and greed.
Drunk on their own hubris.
I saw right through them,
all their lies; all their emptiness.
I had the power to help them...
to save them from themselves.
But it had a price:
The life of the Princess in exchange
for High-Mount's longevity.
Her service and devotion to the one I serve
will be the first of many in the kingdom.
To serve something beyond themselves.
To serve someone with the balls
to purge the evil that lurks in this world.
THAT! Is humanity's true nature!
Placed upon this earth to serve Aibphora!
High-Mount has been primed
and he will guide us all to our true nature."

Could this be true?
Could this devil be right?
Perhaps that Aaron knew.
Their spirits are the same light.

"No... This can't be! You're lying!
The king to forsake his own daughter?
His army could topple you and your demon!"
Aaron yelled in denial as chills grasped his neck;
down to the end of his own spine.

Even while gripping onto what was
left of his hope for his friend's deliverance.
Balaam responded with this in hopes that
Aaron would truly understand:
"I can assure you Aaron, I do not wish to lie to you,
Aibphora wanted one from the Royalty to serve him.
What a better way than to start his reign,
than with the next generation?
To spare the kingdom,
the king and I negotiated that deal.
Indeed, the princess is not dead,
but rather, a convert to **Him**."

Woe! A forced assimilation!
Could this be her end?
A soul for annihilation?
The horror of the end!

The whole dialogue began to spark
something within Elena, but what was it?
A flame? A desire? Yes, a desire to fight,
a desire to stand against this wicked scheme.
She looked over to Aaron,
who was upset about all of it.
The betrayal of his King,
the corruption of his friend.
The theft of his hope and clarity
and all he ever knew growing up.
His own nation, his own king.

Devastated at the revelation.
Elena placed an assuring hand upon
Aaron's shoulder to interceded on his behalf.
Doing so, by telling Balaam off:
"Listen here, I don't care about High-Mount,
or what its fate would be.
But I know this here isn't right.
Your speech on humanity is just bull.
So give us the Princess and piss off."
Balaam responded in a tame manner:
"Or what, serpent?
If you don't care about High-Mount,
then why bother to help him?
Why fight for a lost cause?
You're neither noble nor true, any of you!
None of you are good, for all have their darkness!
Why deny it, why not become it!
You're a monster who only wishes to be human.
All you ever saw was humanity's worst!
Why, you should've joined my cause!"

Is this devil, right?
Are humans truly evil?
Is light the same as night?
This cannot be primeval!

Elena finished her response while
feeling bold in her resolution still:
"Yeah, I am a monster.

And yet, monster or human, I'm still me.
These two have proven you otherwise.
And I'll fight for them to the end!"
Aaron was moved by Elena's words.
Filled with humility, Aaron added:
"Yeah, I want to save the Princess...
And you're right... I do have my shadow.
Everyone does... I wanted glory and wealth.
I wanted it all. I thought I deserved it all, but I..."
Aaron looked at Elena and Eidolon,
now filled with compassion and something
he had longed for since he was a boy,
he couldn't help but give a small and gentle smile
before his two new and dear companions:
"I already have it all.
I have God and my family and companions.
Even if all I have left is the LORD my God,
I'll worship and serve Him as I do now!"

How rich people can be!
Those with family and friends!
They shall rejoice with glee!
For time together is spent!

Eidolon responded with a fire burning within,
to the other two's surprise, by responding:
"Logic of Companions: Sound.
Requirements met.
Enemy logic:

- Flawed
- Contrary
- Destroyed.

Get scraped! Stupid undead, devil want-to-be fool!
HA! HA! HA! HA! HA! HA! HA! HA! HA! HA!"
Such an audience with all they had to say had
made Balaam reach his limit.
At first, he was logical,
then hearing Aaron's devotion to the Lord his God.
Along with the resistance of his companion's against
Aibphora is what made him snap, saying to the three:
"Ap pap pap pap pap pap, shut up shut up shut up,
jus-just shut up. Shut up! SHUT UP! SHUT UP!
I DON'T CARE! Don't you understand you stupid,
bootlicking, arrogant, Blacksmith!?
Sin abounds everywhere and no one's doing anything!
Yet here I am! I'm the one to punish the evil sinners!
Don't you get it? I'M THE SAVIOR HERE! I CARE!
I CARE ABOUT HIGH-MOUNT AN-AND
ENSURING TRUTH AND JUSTICE!! YOUR GOD,
AND HIGH-MOUNT'S ROYALTY HAVE FAILED
TO DO WHAT NEEDED TO BE DONE!!
You, and your Gorgon rip-off and metal tool!
You know what, fuck you Elena!
You should've died that day!
It's better you be limp!
GIVE YOUR CURSE TO ME!
I SHALL COMPLETE MY REVENGE!!"
With his halberd pointed towards Elena,

sludge-like spears struck her arms,
tail, and her heart,
leeching her of her serpentine curse.
Draining her, bleeding her, torturing her.
Screams of agony and pain emerged
deep from within Elena!
Aaron and Eidolon ran to her aid,
only to fail as a giant claw slapped them away.

Like a parasite drinking blood,
So was Elena's curse being taken.
The serpentine in the mud,
a human has now awakened.

There she was, drained, exhausted.
Ragdoll-like as she lay on the stone floor.
A bundle of emotions filled her heart and mind.
From burning to warm to cold and sorrowful.
Swirling and rushing, wave after wave!
Aaron and Eidolon ran to her aid once again.
They looked at and beheld their drained friend.
What's this? Not red scales and claws,
but rather it was olive skin and nails rather than claws!
Where her fangs were, human teeth are now!
Her hair was the same but brunette now.
And her eyes! Not serpentine, but human!
Elena was human! For real this time!
With only rags and Aaron's cloak,
she was vulnerable,

lacking the strength for her bow.
Aaron protected her with his shield.
Balaam bellowed out his triumph:
"You foolish ones!
This was a lost cause the moment you arrived!
You shouldn't have come here at all!
Even now, all is ready for a new era!"
He removed the rags to reveal something monstrous.
His face, once ghoulish is now
fully ghoulish and serpentine!
With a yellow eye once human, serpentine!

Balaam was a hero alright.
More like a fallen hero.
A fallen angel of light,
A heart of absolute zero!

Balaam took his halberd.
Calling upon Aibphora,
"Let us bring justice to a kingdom of gluttons!
To be a kingdom that shall rule all!"
He then struck the ground with his halberd.
The very room began to shake!
The Heroic Misfits began to cling to one another for dear life!
Little did they know what Eckhert Citadel could do!
For between the tree line of the citadel's moat,
fissures opened, and grounds collapsed.
Eckhert Citadel began to rise into the heavens!
Floating towards the Kingdom of High-Mount,

across the forest and across the farmlands.
From below were screams of terror and shock!
Then from the bottom of the citadel's foundations,
came forth giant sludge roots as they struck the earth
with the might of meteors to take root!
Into the palace walls and into the capitol grounds!
"TO ALL THE KINGDOM BELOW!
FROM THIS DAY FORTH,
THERE SHALL BE A NEW ERA!
I SHALL SET THINGS RIGHT!
I HATE YOU AND
ALL YOU STAND FOR HIGH-MOUNT!
I HATE YOU!! I HATE YOU!!
ALL YOU STAND FOR SHALL BURN AND ROT!!"
Balaam and Aibphora yelled in sync.

Filled with malice and hate
was Balaam and Aibphora
One a traitor with hate.
The other a devil of phobia

"All enemies sighted, termination in progress!"
Eidolon said, a fire in his mechanical heart.
"...i-I can... fight, I-" Elena was cut off.
"You need to heal. I won't lose you too..."
Aaron whimpered, anxious and concerned.
Eidolon's arm transformed and began to glow again,
then pointed it towards Balaam.
Only for him to dodge out of range.

Then he returned to his throne.
Shielded in an orange bubble.
"Perhaps, a demonstration will suffice."
Then Balaam pointed to the Princess.
The once petrified Eithne was now moving!
Twitching like that of a possessed ragdoll!
Aibphora used her as if they were one being!
Her entire face, like that of an angler mouth!
With that of claws!
The whole journey a tragedy?

The one Aaron came to save,
A puppet to the traitor!
How will he free the slave?
The blacksmith's heart the greater?

This sludge of Eithne, a puppet, a possession!
"Forgive me dear friend.
For I am powerless!
I have failed you! And our kingdom!"
Eithne thought to herself, like a spectator.
Watching her own body pounce
at her best friend since childhood.
Eidolon intervened with a fist at the angler mouth.
"Release the Princess, cowardly sludge demon!"
Eidolon yelled as fists were being exchanged.
"Fight her, but I beg of you, do not kill her!"
Aaron yelled in what was once concern now agony.
"Affirmative." Eidolon complied.

Balaam and Aibphora watched from
the throne filled with intrigue.

A tragedy is this!
Is this the world's doom?
A friend is missed,
our heroes' tomb?

Eidolon and Eithne fought!
Fire and sludge danced as one was
determined while the other being controlled.
Then the flames have run out!
The other fights with fury for the upper hand.
Slash after slash after slash!
Eidolon now badly damaged,
clawed to near scrap metal!
Clank and Bash they fell.
With Eidolon fallen near Aaron and Elena,
Balaam stood and struck the ground with his halberd.
Then below the three heroes was the void once more!
Swirling around them, sinking like quicksand!
They struggled and struggled to no avail!
Until they were fully consumed below!
With Aaron's hand being the last to go.
"Farewell to the mere misfits," Balaam concluded.

This cannot be the end!
Have the bad guys won?
Will deliverance descent?

All hope cannot be gone!

Meanwhile, in High-Mount below,
were screams and panic all around.
The undead crawling on top of the sludge roots.
They have returned to wreak havoc once more!
This time, the undead differed from last time.
They were thicker in sludge, bones and rot,
with an angler mouth for a face:
The teeth and fangs were red and orange like before.
Some were brute sized, others scrawny,
both of which were 7 feet and taller in height.
With bear-like claws, razor and curved.
Their motive: to kill and convert.
Citizens, fallen and infected.
Converting to undead!
First the royal walls then towards the cities.
The King and Queen and their circle
hid in the cellars, lamenting:
"The kingdom is doomed!"
Some citizens had fought back,
while others had ran away.
Slowly, all of High-Mount will be undead.

Death and chaos all around.
The ghoulish undead had boomed.
To Balaam and Aibphora they are bound.
The Kingdom of High-Mount is doomed!

High-Mount was their first goal,

then their next conquest: the whole world.

"Listen well, Kingdom of High-Mount!

Your judgment and death have come!

With this Citadel,

I shall rule the living and the dead!

All shall know me, and despair!"

Balaam and Aibphora proclaimed in sync.

Aaron's family took refuge in the church.

Protecting those within.

Those who were left.

Some stood guard, others prayed and hoped.

"Wherever Aaron may be, pray that he be safe.

Pray he be delivered.

Then pray that God delivers us through him!"

Father Luke pleaded.

"That stubborn Mijo!

Why has he gone like this!"

Aaron's mother proclaimed in grief.

"He has your heart.

Stubborn he may be,

he never gives up!

And never will... I hope..."

Aaron's father reassured.

As they barricaded the Cathedral,

they continued to guard and pray.

When all seems lost,

there is always hope.

No matter the cost,
never lose hope.

7

HEROES FROM THE ASHES!

There they were, all lying upon the cold obsidian floor.
Aaron thought they died or perhaps worse.
Lying on his side as if he were dead,
Elena was covered in Aaron's cloak on her back,
and Eidolon, badly damaged.
Claw marks all over his metal body.
They all found themselves deep within the bowels
of Eckhert Citadel, near its' foundations.
The hall felt cool, but no frostbite.
No torches, no light, just the bitter cold.
Did they lose the fight?
Did they lose the world? This can't be!
The Princess, a slave to Aibphora!
And the Traitor may as well find his revenge.

Our poor heroic misfits.
They flew close to the sun.
Fallen into the dark pits.
The bad guys have won...

Was I over my head? Was I wrong?
I... I wanted to save Eithne,
I couldn't even do that.
I wanted glory and fortune.
That was a fool's goal.
And now, all suffer for my hubris.
These thoughts tormented Aaron to no end.
His heart beating heavily.
Beating with sorrow for their defeat.
Friends: weakened, broken, possessed.
And here he was, defeated, and desolate.

Weep, you prideful.
For you harvest sorrow.
Weep, you scornful.
For you, there's no tomorrow.

Was joining him a mistake?
To end the hunts after me?
I'm too weak to fight,
wha-what are these!?
My legs? From that state?
Legs which I can't use? A blessing?
A fate worse than what was before?
Tortured by these thoughts and feelings.
Emotions of excitement and confusion and defeat.
Aaron's a hothead, is he courageous or stupid?
I mean... he and Eidolon are the only ones I have since...

Elena had much to process, but so little time.

Loneliness is the worst.
It tricks the brain of everyone.
Was it better to have the curse?
To have and be with no one?

Aaron sat back up slowly.
Saw Elena and weakly crawled to her.
"...Elena?" Aaron called weakly,
now with regained composure,
and with familiar newfound grief,
ones filled with tears and despair.
She crawled towards Aaron in the dark,
holding onto her only friend as she did before:
She crawled towards Aaron in the dark,
holding onto her only friend as she had before:
"I'm so so sorry, dear Elena. I have failed you."
With a damaged arm reached out,
Eidolon said all weakly and shakily:
"priiiiiorityyyyy faiiiiil..."
At this, Eidolon had said their last.
The light of their eyes died out.
Aaron, moved with compassion and guilt,
mourned with Elena at their loss.
With burning skin and insides being jelly,
as they comforted each other in tears.
Within the hour of their deaths.

The poor blacksmith and co.
Enjoying life no further.
They had nowhere to go.
Yet, in the end, had each other.

When all hope seemed lost,
a light appeared within their midst.
A light brighter than the sun!
A figure of silver and gold,
with a blood-soaked robe and eyes of fire.
Surrounded by that of serene flames.
Aaron knew exactly who this was.
Aaron and Elena had covered their eyes
and were on the stone floor terrified and
laid were terrified on the obsidian floor.
"Be not afraid." the figure proclaimed to them.
"Forgive me LORD, for I have failed you!
I am a sinful man who was over his head.
And now the world suffers for my pride!"
Aaron lamented in sorrow and humility.

Our misfits before God,
before him as they are!
They may be flawed,
but they are loved.

This figure, terrifying as before,
spoke firmly yet lovingly:
"Aaron, Aaron, it's not over.

For there's still time. Have you forgotten again?
Your sins have already been forgiven.
High-Mount will know me once again.
I say it to you again:
I am with you, even to the end of the world."
The LORD said unto Aaron.
With those words,
Aaron's heart became full with
the hope and strength to keep going.
To see the calling to the end.

Rejoice you who despair!
Your hearts shall find hope!
For God does truly care,
He is who fulfills your hope!

The LORD then turned towards Elena,
"You suffered greatly, and not a day goes by
where I haven't heard your cries."
Elena cried with intense sorrow
as she choked on her own tears:
"Then why did my parents die!?
Why have that curse upon me!?
You could've...saved them."
The LORD responded to her within her sorrow:
"Your father and mother loved you very much.
Even now, you honor their memory
by helping my servant Aaron. Arise, and walk."
At his word, Elena began to feel something new,

her toes twitched, then her feet, then her legs.
Although it was a struggle initially,
She moved one leg to stand, then the other.
Though wobbly, she could stand for the first time!
In response to this miracle,
she cried on the LORD's shoulder.
This was her thanks to Him,
a contrite, and gentle heart.
Aaron, with a piece of bread, added in,
"I have a little bit left; will this do?"
"Thank you for giving all you have."
Thus said the LORD to Aaron.
He blessed the bread and broke it for them both.
Upon consumption, He vanished from their sight
with renewed strength and hope for victory.

He hears their cries!
In the midst of despair,
the heroic misfits will rise.
For the LORD is there.

"Bendito sea Dios por siempre!" Aaron rejoiced.
As Elena rearranged the cloak into a skirt
(for she was vulnerable from the belly down)
"He's the one you serve?"
"Yes, He appeared to me before,
In the forge of my home.
He made a promise to me,...
So I should stick with Him." Aaron proclaimed.

"What are all of these emotions?
Is this what being human is like?"
"Yep. Trust me, it gets better overtime."
"I've never felt this way about anything,
platonic, romantic, this is all brand new!
I lack the strength for my bow now,
what do I do now?"
Elena questioned with a raw voice.
"Honestly, I'm as confused as you are,
So let's find out together, shall we?"
Aaron resolved mutually.
He then grabbed a small ax from his bag,
then gave it to Elena for her chance to fight,
"It may not be grand, but I hope it helps."

An unorthodox friendship.
Perhaps something more?
Aaron and Elena's friendship,
with love made stronger more.

They looked and beheld their robotic friend.
Beaten and destroyed, yet not totaled beyond repair.
Just a few claw marks that could be welded back.
A destroyed arm. with legs and feet intact,
but not attached to Eidolon's torso intact.
The tank just needs a couple of patches.
"There's gotta be a way to save 'em."
Aaron pondered to himself.
So he looked through his backpack for his tools.

Clank! Bang! Zap! Spark! Slurp! Aaron had to work fast!

Though crudely, Eidolon was repaired!

"sysTEM rebOOTed. Flame fUel DEPLEted."

Eidolon said with a wonky voice.

 "A bit crude, but that'll do for now." Aaron noted.

"It's good to have you back!" Elena said gleefully.

"PriORIties SET. terMINate AIBphora."

Eidolon resolved to the both of them.

Now, Eidolon could only move limply,

so they had to slow down for their torn metal friend.

They had to make their way around the lower levels.

Then resolved to find their way back to the top.

They followed the paths as before,

then once more, found the stairs to the top!

"Ready for the rematch?" Aaron asked boldly.

"Let us save your kingdom!" Elena proclaimed.

"PRIoritY set. HoweVER,

plaCE me DOwn SOMEwhere

thAT I maY covER You."

Eidolon responded.

Back from the dead
are our misfit zeroes!
Their morale is now fed,
Now rise as heroes!

Balaam, sitting on the throne once more.

With his new Serpentine tail coiled upon it.

Princess Eithne, hanging out above

the throne in her new form.
Aibphora proclaimed to Balaam:
"At last! High-Mount shall soon fall,
and we shall take its place.
Soon, after all these years, my revenge
shall be complete and my rule supreme!...
WHAT IS THE MEANING OF THIS!?"
The three of them looked and beheld.
The blacksmith and his companions, alive.
"Argh! Why won't you JUST DIE!?" Balaam yelled.
"Face it Aaron! High-Mount has fallen!
I reign supreme as High-Mount's new king
and the undead shall rule! You have lost!"
Aibphora proclaimed gravely.
"Well we've returned,
and shall put an end to your demonic reign!
High-Mount will be rebuilt!"
Aaron assured, filled with hope and passion.
He drew Caelestis: his trusty sword,
and charged toward the throne,
with Elena following him and Eidolon
being deployed along a pillar as a sentry.

This is the end!
The final battle!
Heroes will ascend!
History shall rattle!

As they charged towards the throne,

The two fiends rocketed up towards the ceiling.

Only for Princess Eithne to be there.

Hanging out upon the throne,

leaped from it like a cat

then landed like a ragdoll:

"I have unfinished business with you, Aaron!"

She cried out with a gravelly voice.

The heroes have stopped in their tracks.

Aaron remained steadfast in his stance and resolve.

Caelestis pointed at the possessed princess.

"Eithne, I don't wanna do this,

but I will stop if you if need be!" Aaron said.

"You're welcome to try!" She shrieked.

At this, she pounced at the heroic man of God.

Slashing and bashing at one another.

A short brawl between friends,

a fight between a brother and sister even.

Aaron parried and slashed as Eithne

was quick on her feet to slash back with her claws.

This would go on until Aaron would sheath

Caelestis then grab his friend by the arm,

Swing her, then shield bash her into submission.

The possessed princess then broke free

to crawled upon the walls.

Out of reach to recover from the fight.

Screeching and scratches from the shadows.

The poor princess,
Trapped in a body.

Possessed princess.
Must save the Lady!

Upon their charge, Balaam and Aibphora vanished.
Upon the roof of the tallest tower of Eckhert Citadel,
They merged into one being as their final act.
They began to transform into something unknown.
Those in High-Mount below looked and beheld,
The sky was orange and black,
changing from day to what was now night!
Clouds swirled around Eckhert Citadel.
Then there it was, a giant Eldritch monster!
With Aibphora's mouth as the entire face.
Its overall length is that of four cedar trees!
The neck itself was long like a cedar tree.
Its body was that of a human torso
with its bottom-half like that of a snake tail.
The length of seven full grown cedar trees!
Its' wings were that of dragon wings,
Big and strong to destroy stone towers!
With four arms like a human,
and the claws like that of a bear!
A roar that could be heard for miles upon miles.

Could this be High-Mount's Apocalypse?
Who could defeat such a monster?
Who is that of an eclipse.
High-Mount's future a blur.

"What is that!?" Aaron yelled, surprised.
"I don't know, but it needs to go down!"
Elena replied equally surprised.
"PriORIty reMAINs the SAme." Eidolon resolved.
"How do we stop it!?" Aaron yelled.
"You're too late!" Eithne yelled,
crawling on what remained of the ceiling.
"From here, the new era shall rise!
With me as its new Queen!"
Then she pounced from above to attack once again!
Everything went silent for all of them.
In that moment, Aaron fell to his knees,
and prayed to his faithful and true God:
"Please, LORD, if it pleases you.
If it fulfills your will,
upon the Kingdom of High-Mount,
shine upon us your light of salvation!"
Then suddenly, when all seemed lost,
crashing from one of the stained-glass windows,
came a device only told in legends, the Arch-wings!
An ancient creation with a wingspan of 21 meters.
The wings were that of eagle wings with
fiery eyes as yellow and golden as the sun,
with words in Hebrew and Greek written all over them.
When it flew, it left a fiery slipstream behind it!
Something even Daedalus would be proud of!
The entry of these majestic and holy wings
blasted Eithne towards the throne knocking her down.
"ARGH!" She yelled gurgled and stunned.

"But how!?" Aaron wondered in delight.
"What is that?" Elena wondered, shocked.
"It's something I was told about in stories,
but it's here! It's actually real!"
Little did Aaron know of its true power.
With it, Aaron could be like that of an archangel.

Ascend you pure-hearted!
Ascend into the heavens!
To finish the race you started!
Perfection filled with sevens!

Where he stood, they fused to Aaron like a weld,
then glowed golden eyes all over him began to glow!
"AwaiTING furTHER stEPS." Eidolon spoke.
Aaron responds:
"Ok, ok, we need to divide and conquer!
I will fight that fiend,
you two free the princess!"
Aaron took off his backpack and gave it to Elena.
"Use whatever I have if it can help!" Aaron said.
Entrusting the contents of his pack to his friends.
He ran and the wings expanded!
His appearance looked immaculate with the wings!
Flying out of the window towards the giant fiend.
Leaving behind that holy and fiery slipstream!
"Be safe, Aaron." Elena whispered to herself.

Our Heroes will fight!

Two below and one will fly!
Against that fiendish freight!
The final battle in the skies!

Aaron soared as a majestic bird in the sky!
Soaring towards the demon's head!
It stopped and hovered in front of Aaron,
who felt like an ant when compared to this giant.
"Your demonic terror ends here!" Aaron yelled.
Filled with a sense of passion and hope.
Balaaibphoram yelled with a thunderous roar,
"I offer utopia! And yet you still resist!?
Very well Aaron of High-Mount,
you shall perish with all of High-Mount below!"
Aaron flew around the flying creature,
always on the attack with a razor slash!
Swooshing and dodging Balaaibphoram with all he had!
Wings flapping like the wind, tail whips like a whip.
In flight Aaron flew and
dodged around this Eldridge creature!
Slashing at its skin as they attempted to smite him!
Like that one fly that cannot be killed.

Into the sky they fly,
Aaron flying like Icarus!
Flying near Heaven on high,
Flying towards Arcturus!

Meanwhile, Elena and Eidolon

could not gaze past the dark clouds.

"Aaron!" Elena yelled.

Eidolon drew their crossbow,

"COMpanion NOT FOUnd. ENEmy deTECTed!"

Then the possessed Eithne got up

and charged towards Elena with claws out!

Balaaiphora sensed the two below to fight.

"Not this again." Elena uttered.

"WhY mUsT yoOu FiGhT?

MuSt yOu WiSh FoR dEAtH

as Aaron does above?"

Elena drew her ax to attack,

"CHANces of VICTory HIGH." Eidolon calculated.

"Don't Be So CERTAIN!" Eithne yelled gravelly.

At this, the fight for her soul was here!

The Fate of the world,

resting upon these three.

The world now swirled.

How will she be free?

Beyond the sky were they:

Aaron vs Balaaibphoram.

The humble vs. the proud.

Michael vs. Lucifer.

Near the border of the Firmament and the Earth.

Balaaibphoram was far from

having any significant damage by Aaron's attacks,

for they continued to soar in the air,

although regenerating their sludge skin.
The hope and passion which filled
Aaron's bones were beginning
to weaken the fiendish monster's might.
"You are more of a threat than I anticipated.
No matter, YOU FIGHT A LOSING WAR!
Your attacks are nothing against me!"
Balaaibphoram yelled in sheer rage.
"Maybe so, but you shall fall before with me!"
Aaron resolved. And so the fight continued,
slash then repair, slash then repair.
Little did Aaron know he had limited time.
For the usage of the Arch-wings can only
last for 7 minutes at a time,
then they depart from the host.
Aaron flew towards Aibphora's jaws.
Aibphora ready to chomp Aaron alive,
SLASH! BANG! CRASH!
Teeth went flying! Within the jaws of death!
Is this how I die? As a demon's main course?
I think not! Perhaps the head shall perish!
Aaron thought to himself as he dived towards
the flying sludge monster's mouth.

Aaron the Blacksmith,
went flying like Icarus!
no one to fight alongside with,
Falling from Arcturus!

Yet, to Aaron's surprise and relief,

he did not find himself inside organs and darkness.

Rather, he found himself inside a round room.

It looked like any other throne room,

but it was surrounded with these

grand statues of a singular person.

A handsome figure, yet something about it was off.

They all had the same features of an angler mouth,

yet the eyes of the man were still there.

"You should've taken the offer you know."

A voice called out from the shadows.

"I've had enough of this.

Show yourself!" Aaron yelled.

Then, from one of the statues,

Balaam strikes from behind,

only for Aaron to parry with his shield.

This time he appeared as before,

but with no serpentine curse nor undead features,

he appeared human and goodly with raven black hair

and ivory skin with brown eyes.

Yet he wore those same tattered clothes and armor.

Armed with his double headed halberd.

This time, they were divided for duel-wielding.

"Impressive, but not enough.

You're still that bum with nothing.

You're way over your own head!"

Balaam growled full of his ego and hubris.

So this is where it all ends.

A duel of an angel and demon.
Yet one can make amends.
The other, condemnation!

At the same time,
he was envious and outraged by
Aaron wearing the Arch-wings.
Why is he champion? Balaam thought to himself.
Things were finished properly when I was champion.
Why him of all people?
Balaam pondered as he continued to witness
Aaron with the Arch-wings shining and burning
with all of its heroic and blazing glory.
"This was me before I became what I became.
As I have told you before, I tell you once again.
I wanted what was right but no one else wanted it.
I did what everyone, including your God,
was too afraid to do. So I did it all myself!
They all deserved death, they all deserved Hell.
I will exterminate all who stand against me,
against all whom I hate! Especially you!
Do you really thing some pair of wings can stop me?
You're nothing but a piece of shit without them!
You aren't even worth a damn! Lower than dirt even!"
Balaam yelled to discourage Aaron.
"Says the bozo who sold his soul away!
If what you say is true,
then I will fight to protect all that you hate!"
Aaron replied smugly yet with conviction

deep from within his heart.
The fire within Balaam's eyes ignited once more:
"Piss off ya fucking bootlicker! Have at you!"
With Caelestis and shield in both hands,
Aaron took his stand and knew what he
must do if he was to save High-Mount.
To save all the people of the kingdom below,
his Church, his family, his childhood friend Eithne,
and his two companions who helped him this far:
His mechanical friend Eidolon,
and Elena his monster friend who he loves dearly.
"You said once that your name will haunt me.
I wanted my name to be known to all.
But not anymore. I am sure of this:
May the LORD's name be glorified above all names!
So bring it on!"

A duel shall commence.
A duel of an angel and demon.
This be the angel's penance?
To fight against a lemon.

Balaam delivered the first blow.
Aaron shielded with his trusty shield
then counter-attacked with Caelestis!
CLASH! SLASH! BASH! CLASH! BASH!
SLASH! CLASH! SLASH!
Then came the test of might between
hardened steel and burning corium!

Between a blacksmith of heaven and a soldier of hell!
Between a saint and an apostate!
Aaron was firm with the Arch-wings.
Not only did the Arch-wings grant its host
the abilities of super-strength and flight.
It protected its wielder from all harm and recoil.
Aaron cannot be harmed!
Then came the test of might!
What was seconds felt like minutes, but what's this!
Balaam still overpowers Aaron,
slowly losing his stance.
Then something, Someone!
Was holding Aaron on his feet!
"I-Impossible! He should be knocked down by now!
Divine intervention? Now that's just cheating!"
Balaam thought to himself.
If that is you, Holy Spirit, that is protecting me,
then thank you dear friend.
Aaron was not sure in his brain,
but in his heart he knew.
Aaron pushed and he pushed
until he got the upper hand!
Pushing Balaam back to the center of the circular room.
Then Aaron saw his opening:
BASH! SLASH! SLASH! At then STAB!
Went Caelestis right into Balaam's abdomen!
Then slashed out to expose
masses of blood and a few organs.
Yet, Balaam stood remaining firm on his feet!

To ensure his victory over Balaam,
Aaron sliced Balaam's right arm clean off!
Then a slice to the chest and STAB!
Right through the heart!

A living dead.
A dying life.
A life he bled.
Destroying his life.

Meanwhile, within Eckhert Citadel's throne room,
Eithne was fighting with all her might.
While Elena and Eidolon fighting with all they had left,
"ARGH!" Eithne yelled in agony,
a chunk of sludge fell from her,
Eithne backed away from the two heroes,
as the sludge clanged to her.
She resisted, striving to rip Aibphora
off of herself chunk by chunk.
One had tried to gather them, the other to separate.
Until all fell away from the princess.
Then with Elena assisting in tearing the sludge off,
broke the princess from her possession! Free at last!
There the princess lay, blacked-out and weary.
Elena and Eidolon triumphant yet weary themselves.
"AnALYalysis reqUIRED." Eidolon replied.
Elena examined her heartbeat on her neck.
Then laced the blade of her ax to her nose,
then discovered her weak breathing.

"She's alive, we need to go, now!" Elena said.

"PRIority FULfilled..." Eidolon replied assuredly.

The Princess is free at last!
Aibphora's sludge fallen away,
away from the heroes fast,
to return on another day.

The living death now a dying life,
Balaam was petrified where he stood.
Like a breathing statue.
Yet this be his final words to Aaron,
Champion of High-Mount:
"You did it...You defeated me... Once and for all...
but mark my words... I may fall... but the Princess...
She'll take my place... If you be... God's Champion...
Then Eithne... Shall be Aibphora's... Champion...
...I was, the best one... But... You... are not me... Are you?"
At this, he breathed his last, just standing there.
A hero who died a tragic villain, damning himself.
"You could've been great,
yet your pride and rage
consumed your Corazón.
So... yeah. Maybe we are the same..."
Aaron thought as he took off
his helmet to bid Balaam a farewell
as he escaped the collapsing room.
The young man who had left the kingdom
as a hot-headed blacksmith and laughingstock

has now returned as its hero.

Aaron and Balaam.
Two sides of one coin.
One did give a damn.
The other couldn't join.

Elena could only carry the weakened princess.
With Eidolon to provide cover with just one arm.
They had to make their way out of Eckhert Citadel,
by sliding down one of the sludge roots
onto the tallest tower of Brackenridge Palace.
Then Elena decided to hold onto Eidolon and Eithne
as they slid on Eidolon down the root.
Weakly, Eithne regained consciousness as they slid.
"...w- Wha? Who...are you?" She asked softly.
 "Some companions to Aaron." Elena responded.
"PRIoriTY set: EscORT prinCESS to SAFEty."
Eidolon concluded when the three reunited at
High-Mount's tallest tower
right beneath the floating citadel.
"...what about... Aaron?"
Eithne asked still weakened.
Then from the sky, they looked and beheld.
The falling Balaaibphoram
with Aaron in the broken teeth,
"AARON!" Elena yelled in horror.
Aaron was struggling to escape, 30 seconds to impact.
"Come on, break free!" Aaron muttered to himself.

25 seconds, 20 seconds, 15 Seconds, 10 SECONDS!!
Then, just as teeth and sludge and blood
splattered everywhere, Aaron broke free,
with wings spread and fire trailing!
Balaaibphoram's body crashed and shook the earth
near the farmland of the kingdom!
Shaken to their foundations,
yet but did not tremble and collapse!
That demonic sludge, slain in defeat.
Now recollecting himself to retreating
for another time.

The impossible has occurred!
a mere blacksmith and friends,
saved the princess, now cured!
The world, saved from the fiends!

Aaron, hovering where he was at,
saw his friends in the tower,
and proceeded to fly over to them.
With only one minute to make it.
He flew as swiftly as he could towards
Brackenridge Palace to his companions.
30 seconds, 25 seconds, 20, 15, 10 SECONDS LEFT!!
Almost there... he thought to himself.
Soaring like a comet towards them.
9, 8, 7, 6 the time flew with Aaron.
As he approached the one tower of the palace.
With his three friends on top.

5, 4, 3, 2, 1, at that Aaron had landed in time
just before the wings detached.
Aaron stumbled on the landing,
but regained his composure.
Now the Arch-wings hovered above them,
like a vulture circling around its prey.

Like Icarus our hero fell.
And yet our hero lives.
Do not wish our hero hell,
For instead, pray that he lives.

He beheld his three friends, especially her.
"Eithne?" He asked somberly.
"...Aaron..." Eithne said weakly.
Aaron then embraced the three of them.
"...thank you..." Eithne thanked.
"What do we do now?" Elena wondered.
"HEALing reqUIRED." Eidolon explained.
Aaron looked down below,
to see the undead in High-Mount.
All of them, still remained and are running rampant.
Now with a new goal in mind:
To go to the palace and slaughter the Heroic Misfits.
"One last thing to finish..." Aaron said.
He looked up towards the Arch-wings
as it hovered above them and Eckhert Citadel.
"I have used up my time with the Arch-wings,
But I'll hold them off!" Aaron said boldly.

"...Thank you...I can...die...
with my...friends...then..."
Eithne said faintly.
Who now can fly with these wings?

At last, friends reunite.
Yet there was no joy.
For the Citadel was in site.
Looming and waits to destroy.

Something awakened within Elena.
Something new, something... divine?
Whatever it was, it tugged at her.
What is this emotion? A drive?
I felt it from before, Aaron felt it too!
It's got to be! Well, here goes nothing.
She knew what she needed to do,
so she got on her knees and prayed:
"Please, God of Aaron and his Church,
let me help you both. One last time!"
At this simple desire, this simple act of faith,
the Arch-wings flew down to her, giving her flight!
With its golden fire and eyes glowing all over her,
how invigorating it was! To be filled with joy and hope!
"You helped me, Aaron. So let me help you!"
She proclaimed, with vigor and hope in her heart.
"Wai-wha-what? What are you-" Aaron stuttered.
Elena embraced him with a hug one last time.
Then turned to Eidolon and shook their hand.

"IT has beEN AN HOnor." Eidolon croaked softly.
She flew towards the hoard with ax in hand.
And slayed them like wheat in a field.
With a hand-wave, she pulled out a bow,
many grand and fiery arrows flew
and struck all the hoard in her path.
In just a matter of two minutes,
every undead laid slayed in her path.
Then she took to the sky leaving the fiery slipstream.
And with the might of Behemoth,
Elena struggled to uproot the entire citadel.
Dirt and sludge and stones were being ripped
from the ground as the earth
shook with a mighty earthquake!
Then rip and torn it went!
Uprooted from where it floated above High-Mount!
With all that she had,
she took the citadel far up and up and up!
Far beyond the firmament and into outer space.
She then swung it around like a tether ball,
feeling light in her hands,
she threw the dreadful citadel right into the sun!
Floating and hurtling towards it,
Eckhert Citadel burned and scorched,
then at last disintegrated.

When all seemed lost,
A blacksmith and snake saved the day!
With their lives crossed,

High-Mount will see the next day!

Elena then flew down to her friends.
The Arch-wings disconnected from her,
then it proceeded to fly up into the sky.
Elena then fell to her knees from exhaustion.
"The day is won?" Aaron said weary.
"PpriORITYority fulFILLEDfilled..." Eidolon stated.
Aaron approached Elena and held onto each other.
"We won... It's over..."
Aaron stated as both began to weep.
Eithne, holding onto Eidolon, joined them both.
What remained of the guard surrounded them.
"Shall I give the order?" One guard asked the King.
"No. Leave this to me. Leave us." The King ordered.
"...father?" Eithne looked at him.
At this, the guards complied.
The king said nothing to Aaron.
Only to embrace Princess Eithne.

Here were the four.
Tired and weary.
After all the blood and gore,
now felt dreary.

8

— · —

THE VICTORY WITH NO CHEER.

The following Chapter will show what truly happens in the end of this story which cannot be shown through the poetic structure. Instead, it will be presented in regular form.

The King had took in Princess Eithne, and kicked the Heroic Misfits out of the castle. He wanted to arrest and execute them. And yet, they did save Eithne. Even if he ordered their arrest, he just couldn't do it. So much loss, so much destruction, all at his footstep. The Royal Guard was weakened. So, he just decided to kick them out, they couldn't tell what he was telling them through such as gesture. Was it a simple "Get out!" or was it a "Thank you…?" something only the Princess would know.

There was just silence between the three of them. All shell-shocked and humbled at heart. All that pain was too heavy for a single word. Once they were out of the castle walls and back in the ruined city, just nothing. All Aaron could think of after knowing Eithne was safe, was the Cathedral and his family. So, Aaron decided to just go there in silence, with Elena and Eidolon to join him.

Everywhere they went, the streets that were once filled with life and business was now in ruins. Filled with the poor souls of those who had fallen to the claws and jaws of Balaaibphoram's undead hordes. Some bodies and areas polluted the air with that blazing invisible force which was too contaminated to either walk into or be nearby.

The bodies were just left to rest there in the streets, lifeless, as the maggots and fungi ate away at their corpses. After a while, they finally saw the Cathedral and moved slower and slower, then all three collapsed. Aaron's father peaked out one of the openings from one of the bell towers to see his own son collapsed on the ground with a girl and a mechanical knight. He was moved with compassion to see his son return! He informed some inside to go out with him to retrieve the collapsed heroes. Aaron's father and his oldest sister, along with a couple of other folks brought them all in.

The Heroic Misfits could finally rest safely while in the house of the Lord. While Aaron and Elena rested, Aaron's parents decided to repair Eidolon as best they could.

Identities: Unknown. However, Aaron sees them as what he calls 'family.' What is family? They do not desire harm against me. If they are Aaron's, they are mine too.

Eidolon thought to himself, consenting to their offer of repairing him. Clank! Spark! Bash! Ding! Clank they went! At least one arm and both legs were rebuilt (the other arm still damaged), the torso was temporarily patched. The mechanical knight's voice would have to be restored to its original state once they had access to their workshop. And as thanks for helping Aaron, Father Luke gave Eidolon a blue stash with the family crest.

A few days went by in the Kingdom of High-Mount,

Aaron and his loved ones were still there in the Cathedral. His parents and Father Luke were just outside the room where he and Elena were in.

In separate beds, it was Elena who would be the first to awakened, she saw her friend fast asleep across the room. "...Aaron?" She softly asked while groggy. Aaron moaned: "w-hat?" he slowly awakened also in a groggy state: "...elena? W-hat is it?" His parents were alarmed at the voice and rushed inside the room. Now that they were awake, they had so many questions. Such as 'who was this girl that Aaron brought back with him?' It was clear to them that she cared for him, it was finally time for Elena to officially meet his parents. "Who are you?" They interrogated. Elena told them: "Please, don't cast me out. I am a friend to Aaron, and Elena is my name." Although she was hesitant to say more, she figured if she could trust Aaron, then she could trust his parents. So she confessed:

"I was the Serpent of the Woods. I was the one that everyone wanted to kill and have me as a trophy. That was until I met your son. I thought he was another hunter, but he proved to me otherwise. He proposed that we worked together to save the Princess so I can have my name cleared... I never thought it would lead to me becoming human."

They were both surprised at this. "Wait a minute... It can't be... You're her!" Aaron's father discovered. "Wait, what?" Elena asked all surprised. "Yes! Your parents were old friends of ours, they may have been above us, but they didn't fear us. They left it all behind to protect you. How can this be?" Aaron's father wondered fully puzzled.

All the memories of her family, all the joy and sorrow she had to face, to learn what led up to now, just washed over her at the mere mention of her parent's. "Yep. I actually had the curse taken away from me. The one who betrayed your kingdom was the one that cursed me. AND it was your son who took him down." Elena explained. "You mean..." Aaron's mother interjected. "Yes, your son is a hero...and my hero too." Elena said as she looked at him with a sparkle in her eye and a small yet genuine smile. They were shocked yet impressed when they heard all that Aaron had done. How they both met and how they protected her home. How they repaired and be-friended Eidolon. How they entered Eckhert Citadel and into the void. She did not speak about when Aaron was confront-ed by Aibphora, for that was only his to tell (he didn't talk much about what happened during that encounter). How she overcame Balaam and nearly froze to death. How they united to stop Balaaibphoram. Most importantly, how God himself healed and helped the three of them save the Princess, and by extent the entire kingdom (and potentially the entire planet). They could not have been prouder than they have always been!

***

A few more days had passed, and Elena did not leave Aaron's side. Aaron would go to the Cathedral to meet up with Father Luke to tell him all that had happened, and Elena was with him at this particular time. The once jaded eyes that gazed upon him a couple of weeks ago were now a renewed hope. "Father I-" Father Luke interrupted: "No... It is I who should be thanking you. The LORD our God has delivered our kingdom through you. Both of you." Aaron and Elena got to tell Father Luke about all that had happened within the walls of Eckhert Citadel. Especially for Elena when she was in the liminal place and how she was rescued, then how the LORD appeared to her and Aaron. "..." "Well? Did I miss anything?" She asked a little intimidated (keep in mind she has very little friendly human interaction outside of Aaron, his family, Eidolon, and her deceased parents). "No...Truly, the both of you have been blessed. May you both go in peace, glorifying the LORD by your lives." With this, Aaron and Elena had left the Cathedral to now visit Princess Eithne.

Upon being allowed to see her, something didn't feel right, was she in a coma? Was this the after-effects of all the trauma and fighting? The last one cannot be, because Elena and Aaron had been through the same yet different experiences too! She has been slowly weakening over the last few days and yet was not dead. All their medicines did not work, what was causing it? So, they requested to bring Father Luke in as a last resort. Once there, he knew exactly what was happening. "I'm afraid this is no ordinary coma. I sense that it is that demon's doing! I've seen it before, the only thing we can do for her now is pray and fast. She will need a lot of willpower to escape this." So some of them prayed for her while others fasted, but only a few did both.

Within her trance, Eithne found herself in a dream state. It was more like a nightmare really. She found herself in High-Mount. But something felt wrong. She looked around, everyone she knew. All... dead. Her family fell with many stab wounds as well as bites and claw marks. She explored more and more of the castle and the overall town. Aaron was found hanging by his neck from the top of one of St. Gabriel Cathedral's bell towers. Elena was also hung by her neck on the other bell tower. The metallic smell of blood and guts were all over the place; Blood and sludge in the ground and all around her. This tortured her to no end to witness everything around her. All her loyal subjects and all her family and friends. All whom she could not to save. *"No no no nonononono."* Eithne cried out while distraught. Weeping and gnashing her teeth.

Then there was that maniacal and gravel laughter. **"Oh, what a tragedy."** The voice asked.

Then Eithne slowly looked behind and up towards the familiar voice. It was him once more. Aibphora as he was before the fusion. **"Your heroes may have won the day, but you cannot smite me down! In the light, and in the shadows, I AM A PART OF YOU! I am yours and you are mine! You and I are one!"** He boomed sinisterly and maliciously with a passionate roar.

"n-NO! We won; he stabbed your core! Both of you fell!" Eithne shrieked with dread.

"OH how wrong you are *Princess*. I am a part of all that live. As long as life goes on, I will haunt and torture and HATE all who live. Mark my words *Princess*, as long as you live, I will haunt you. I will be within your heart, a part of your being. Torture you. TO BREAK YOU AND DRAG YOUR SOUL TO HELL!! Maybe, you're already there..."

He then drew his claws to attack. Knowing it was a fight she could not win, Eithne covered herself via duck and cover. Closing her eyes as if death was to snatch her away right then and there, to deliver her to eternal torment that was, the maggots and flames. Aibphora floated towards Eithne, raised then claw AND THEN- ...Eithne awakened within the castle walls...

***

Fast forward a year and a half later, High-Mount had toiled and labored to restore the kingdom to its former state. Yet times shall never be as it were before. All the farmlands had to be refilled, the sludge had ruined portions of the farmlands of wheat and other crops. All of High-Mount's people had to contribute to its clean up. Some were drafted, while others volunteered to endure the heat which the blobs were emitting. Many died or had chronic illnesses directly related to the cleanups. Though the active threat was over, the famine still flourished. Then one day, the rains had returned to the land. Drop after drop and downpour after downpour. The uncontaminated land flourished once more.

Now, the cleanup of the contaminations went like this: They had to dig open the ground to separate the lands. Next, they created walls to isolate the sludge-covered farmland.

As for the capital itself, they had to clean out the streets of what remained of the corpses and all the blood and sludge. The streets were swept and control-burned to purify it of any demonic presence. Bones were gathered to be piled and burned in respect for those that had fallen and to mourn them. Walls were repaired, furniture replaced.

As for the St. Gabriel Cathedral, the inside was intact, but its exterior and a few windows were broken. While the Church of the Holy Ingot and the district it resided in took a majority of the damage alongside Brackenridge Castle. As the famine was slowly being relieved by the rain. Aaron's family and Eidolon were among the many who volunteered to help in the cleanup process.

A year after the day of the ghoulish invasion. There was a decree from the Royal Court to make it a day of mourning, that High-Mount never forget the ones they lost that day. For Aaron as well as his family and friends, it was a day of fasting and silence. A day to remember how the LORD delivered the Kingdom of High-Mount from death and from the end of the world.

Princess Eithne did not want to suffer everything she had been through again. So, she decided to learn how to fight, courtesy of Aaron's family, though not a soldier at heart, she would know how to defend. In the workshop's testing room ,she was dressed in a work-styled kirtle and equipped with two daggers. Stab after slash after bash at a testing scarecrow. This went on for one day out of the week whereas the rest of the week was dedicated to royal duties. Her nightmares were of that day, the day she was captured. How helpless and trapped she felt. It replayed in her head again and again! Memories of Aibphora possessing her like a ragdoll. His words echoed in her head again and again:

"I am a part of all that live. As long as life goes on, I

haunt and torture all who live. I will haunt and torture you *Princess*."

Though these nightmares remain, she was determined to not let that fiend consume her. To not let herself take Balaam's place as Aibphora's play-thing. She will be ready if the kingdom was attacked again. Especially if **HE** were to attack again.

Eidolon received a few upgrades. Alongside the repairs he was given before, his crossbow arm was now repeating! All that Eidolon had to do was to retract the bow after each shot and a new arrow was loaded and ready from a box that would be fed from beneath the crossbow! His Greek Fire hand now has a backup container. That's right, not one but two containers were equipped. Though the backup is smaller than the primary, Eidolon had more firepower in case the occasion arose for its' necessity. As thanks for assisting in the rescue of Princess Eithne, Eidolon was dubbed as a sentry to Aaron's Family. As for Elena, she found the help she needed from her past traumas. Though they will always be a part of her, she was given better ways to cope. Such as her continuation of archery and a lute to vent her frustrations. Though she has grown accustomed to her new-found humanity, she was still rather wobbly when she walked. Perhaps it could have had to do with how she always slithered that such wobbling stuck with her.

***

A year and a half after the ghoulish invasion, the Heroic Misfits were summoned to the King's Court. All three had to testify about all that had happened. It was here that Elena confessed to the Council:

"You all know me, yet no one here knew me. You all wanted me dead, but here I am. I was the Serpentine of the Woods that many hunted for."

The whole Council was shocked at the news. One responded, "How can this be? You're a human?" Another responded, "If you truly are who you claim to be, then you should be hung!" Elena remained unflinching at the comments towards her:

"I was the one who slaughtered those who were sent to hunt me down. They invaded my home, I had to defend it! For there was a curse placed upon me while in my mother's womb. It was given to me as an act of revenge upon my parents. For their loyalty to you, your majesty, by turning over the Traitor. It was the Traitor and the mob that was sent all those years ago. They were those who slayed my parents, I had to avenge them! For years I lived with this memory... The guilt... I also helped Aaron of High-Mount in saving the princess and defeating the Traitor and the Demon... and well, here I am."

Elena shrugged off and expected comments to be given. Then Aaron, Eidolon, and Princess Eithne vouched for Elena and her testimony to confirm them true. Aaron came forth and spoke:

"She speaks truthfully, your highness. We met on her grounds, though unintentionally. We were under attack and worked together to repel the undead. She and I came unto an agreement to stop the traitor together in exchange to clear her name and end the hunts against her. Then we encountered our mechanical friend Eidolon rusting away. We repaired them and the three of us went to save your daughter, your highness."

Aaron testified. No one would dare a word against him after hearing rumors of him fighting Balaaibphoram. Including the Patron from before, for he was still bitter about Aaron's punch to the jaw. So, Aaron continued:

"There were many horrors and nightmares we had to face if it meant saving the Princess. But we were already too late by the time we reached her. All we knew what that the sludge demon possessed and physically corrupted her from head to toe."

The queen questioned: "If what you have claimed is true, then how is she standing before us as she was before?" Aaron, though patient with the questions did respond:

"The truth is, we didn't know, your highness. We didn't know how to save her. All we knew was that the traitor and the demon needed to be stopped. IF they were stopped, then hopefully it would've freed her... Turns out we were right."

Eithne did not say anything, it was still recent for her. Too much to bring up herself. As for the rest of Council, some were just confused and sat there. Others just leaned forward in their chairs intrigued by the testimony they all just heard. "You mean to suggest that you placed the fate of High-Mount's Princess, my daughter, on a guess?" The King asked rather indignant.

Although Aaron was hesitant to present to the Council the King's betrayal, he figured that he never needed to be afraid to do what was right. Especially after all he had been through.

"And do you, the King, mean to suggest that every member present, with the exception of the Queen, entrusted the King- dom's longevity on a deal with the traitor who attacked us?"

As they heard that accusation. Some were shocked, others were insulted at the fact that our heroes discovered the secret that would tear them down if word got out. "This is nonsense, I'm innocent!" one councilmember yelled. "Even if that were true, you have no proof!" said another councilmember. "Yes, it was to our dismay that there is evidence against you for bribery and treason against the Kingdom of High-Mount!" The council had gasped and muttered to themselves at the last statement. "Preposterous! Not only do you have me mourn my daughter before us, but you also dare accuse me before everyone here of betraying my own kingdom!?" The king roared angrily.

"The writing's on the wall your highness." Aaron replied just standing there firmly yet behind his green eyes was terrified. Princess Eithne stepped in to intervene on Aaron's behalf and vouch boldly with a pain in her heart:

"It is true father; we have before you a contract stating that you would sell me to the traitor's demon in exchange for High-Mount's protection. On it has your name with a handwriting I know too well, along with your seal!"

At this, the king remembered the contract and could not hide his guilt as the Council murmured to themselves. He had straightened himself:

"Very well, to my Council and my Kingdom it is true! I have made a deal that would jeopardize us all! If I refused his deal, no one would be standing here today. I did what needed to be done for the good of the kingdom. But know this Aaron, the kingdom will never know of this. For history will know you and those you love as traitors with me as the one who snuffed them out! Take them away!"

At this the King snapped his fingers to summon the guards to take Aaron and his two companions away to be forgotten and tortured. That was until the Queen intervened to stop the king. "HALT!" She yelled. "The final sentence needs both of our votes. And I veto their arrest. Will the Council veto their arrest and vote on the arrest and dethroning of the King?" A majority of the councilmembers voted against the impulse arrest. Yet they were all conflicted about the final part. Instead, they voted against the arrest of the Heroic Misfits and saved the King's fate for the end of the trial.

Now it was up to the Queen to hear the trial rather than the king. "Very well then. Let these three finish their testimonies. Now please, speak your peace Eidolon, Knight of Metal!"

At this Eidolon identified themself and testified:

"Name: Eidolon.

Creator(s): Unknown.

Alliances: Aaron of High-Mount, Elena, and Princess Eithne of High-Mount.

Current Priorities: None

Past Priorities:

-   Terminate Aibphora

-   Terminate Traitor of High Mount

-   Save Princess of High Mount." Eidolon testified and continued in smooth and metallic voice:

I was awakened by Aaron and Elena, who repaired my damage and dull weaponry. We found our destination: The Eckhert Citadel. I was then consumed by the sludge and burned it alive. Then I was reunited with my companions and sought after set priorities. We failed to fulfill them. However, the circumstances of the situation helped us succeed."

Princess Eithne was up next to testify before the council and her own family. So she proceeded:

"To my Father and Mother: The King and Queen of High-Mount. The day I was captured, I remember awakening in a throne room like the one we're in now. Then I was being consumed by the sludge of the demon. I tried to break free, but it was no use. Then before I knew it, all I saw was darkness... I felt consumed, hopeless, and terrified... I wasn't myself. I was... I was being controlled... My body was possessed by the sludge. I could see everything, but had no control! I fought Elena and Eidolon against my own will. Then I remembered pain and a melting sensation... Then I was... me again. Weakened and worn, Elena and Eidolon took me back to safety here on the castle's tower. Then, weirdly, Aaron and Elena both had wings brighter than the sun and fire followed them. The Traitor and all of Eckhert Citadel fell and were destroyed."

The entire Court was shocked and muttered among themselves.

As for the Queen, she sat there on the throne. Thinking. Puzzling. Pondering. Calculating. Then she stood up and spoke to everyone present:

"It seems these four are speaking the truth. There is blood on Elena's hands, and yet she has shown redemption in saving our daughter. If she truly is guilty even of one crime against the kingdom, then by my scepter I declare you, Elena, pardoned of any and all charges against you."

And so, Elena knelt before the queen and was dubbed by the scepter. The queen then turned to Aaron and pardoned him:

"As for you, Aaron of High-Mount, you once came here as a blacksmith and left here on a suicide mission. It was foolish of you... At the same time, you came home with my daughter, the princess, alive... You came back as a hero... I declare you pardoned of any and all charged against you."

Aaron knelt before the Queen as well and she proceeded to dub him with her scepter. As for the King, the majority of the council were conflicted since some were there when it happened. 2/3 of the council had decided to vote the King guilty of bribery and treason. Some did it in hopes of redemption, others to not get caught for their fair-share of activities.

At the Queen's orders, the guards rushed in and arrested the King. He struggled and struggled as they dragged him away. "Wai-what are you doing! You can't do this to me! I have the crown! Without me, the Kingdom of High-Mount is doomed! We're all gonna die if I'm dethroned! We'll only collapse like all the other kingdoms, BECAUSE OF YOU!"

The king concluded as he was dragged out of the throne room as the doors shut.

With the crown on the throne, the queen then proclaimed. "With no king, there must be a ruler for High-Mount. With the Council's approval, I shall take the King's place as the Queen of High-Mount. Does the Council veto?"

At this, the Council paused in silence after their murmuring. They all decided on the Queen as High-Mount's head leader with a 2/3rds approval from the Council. With this, the Queen took the crown and held it up before the council and all held their hands before their hearts as a pledge. The Queen proceeded to take her place up on the King's throne and placed the crown upon her head.

***

The three of them were free! After all this was over and her name cleared, Elena had decided that she wanted to leave. Aaron was true to his word since Elena was true to hers. Aaron, his family, Eidolon, and Eithne were outside of the city gates as they bid her a proper farewell. "Thank you, all of you." Elena said bittersweetly. "May the LORD my God watch over you as He watches over me." Aaron replied. They both embraced with a hug. Eithne and Eidolon joined in as well. "Thank you for saving me. May you live in peace." Eithne blessed. "Permanent Friend added: Elena. May we meet again." Eidolon said. With this, Elena made her journey home to the Forest of Iniquity.

As she made it home, everything was where she left them. Yet...nothing was the same. She unpacked what she was given. One day, she sat at the spot where she first met Aaron, to watch the waterfall of her pond and reflect upon everything. She thought about the curse, she about her parents, then of Aaron and Eidolon, then of Eckhert Citadel with all she had to endure there. Then her encounter with Aaron's God and the liminal space with color from above, and then the Arch-wings. So many memories, some good, some bad.

A couple of months have gone by. She carried on as she did before the adventure. Yet, nothing could be as it were before. She just couldn't shake off all those memories. So, she concluded: Why did I come back here? There's nothing left here for me now!" So, she packed a few things and left this former home of hers. "I'll never forget this place." She said with a melancholic look. With this, she returned to High-Mount.

As for Aaron, things were never the same for him either. He is a blacksmith, but also the LORD's Champion for High-Mount. One day he went outside of the city gates and into the farm fields. The ones which he once ran through for the rescue. He did this so he could think and reflect on his own thoughts. He thought of his encounters with the LORD, he thought of Eckhert Citadel, the encounter with Aibphora. He thought of his dear friends Elena and Eidolon. Though Eidolon is now a part of Aaron's family as a sentry, he also missed Elena dearly and truly loved her. He questioned if the LORD's promise to him came true by just one event. So, he thought:

He said that High-Mount will know Him once again. What does that mean after all that happened? Has it come true yet? Did we win? Did I blow it? Was I the hero or a blunder? Well I will still worship and serve Him anyway. It would be amazing if I could see Elena again. Just once...

As he was about to turn back home, a figure was in the distance. He squinted to see who it was. Then he knew, it was her! Elena!

He then proceeded to walk which turned into a run. With tears in both their eyes, they embraced each other. They then proceeded back to the city gates together. It was from that time onward that she did not have to live so cold or alone in the Forest of Iniquity anymore! She has a new home, and friends who will have her back. No more hiding, no more being hunted! Alongside Eithne in her training, Elena took up archery again. As thanks for helping Aaron, his parents crafted her a new bow made just for her now that she was human. She even helps in the hunt for the Festival of Falling Leaves! Many were impressed.

As for where both Aaron and Elena would go from there, they grew fondly of each other. They have been through so many valleys and darkness. And yet, they made it through with an unwavering friendship.

In fact, they both saw in their hearts that it was good. In three years' time since she came back, they courted one another. For Aaron to be Elena's husband, and Elena to be Aaron's wife. How joyful that day was for them both! There in the Church, they vowed. Through the hills and valleys of life, they would learn and grow and love together. Fulfilling their promises to the end of their days. There was much rejoicing and cheering and feasting, courtesy of Princess Eithne. Finally, Aaron was still the Church's New Champion. In the meantime, he found peace with his lot in life. As a blacksmith. Of course, until he is called again to fulfill his duty to the Lord his God.

With a family and a wife who love him. And so, some of his achievements were recognized by the public as a town hero. Though he did not know it, there were some who came to the faith since the day of the ghoulish invasion. But to Aaron, he was content with that. A quiet and fulfilling life where he is, was worth living. Even though he, like Eithne, suffered the nightmares inflicted upon him by Aibphora. He could still face them knowing that the LORD is greater.

Though Balaam and Aibphora are defeated, Aibphora was still lurking in the shadows. With that dreadful citadel destroyed. Aibphora now has to lurk and roam around the kingdom, around the world if it was necessary. And yet, a piece of him was still within her. Through Eithne, maybe he could get his revenge. Inside of her, he can see within the castle walls.

He can read her thoughts, her heart. He could morph her once more into what she was. Oh yes, a wet dream come true for the damned fiend! If God had His champion, then he would create another champion within the princess to rival Aaron and tear him down. Making him a laughingstock, once again, and rub it in God's face!

"Such blind fools, I offered them paradise, to serve me and live forever. Where one embraces death and thrives in it. It's such a shame they continue their avarice and pride. No matter, with my servant destroyed, I will find my revenge. Whether it be soon, or a thousand years from now, I shall remain resolute, that *blacksmith* and those with him I shall haunt. Yessss. Eithne... She shall be my champion. Through her, they shall know. All shall know me, and what it means to DESPAIR."

And so, Aibphora had to plan something. Something worse than before, something... Diabolical, sinister, perhaps increases the scope of the scheme. All he knew what that Eithne was the key. Aaron of all people shall be worse off for it. He had in mind to torture Aaron the most. Obsessing over it until it was done. If he is preparing his revenge, then so will Aaron and those with him to be ready for it. But that will be a story for next time...

THE END

— · —

ABOUT THIS BOOK

*H*igh-Mount's Champion* first started as a creative writing essay I wrote way back in 2017 during Junior Year of High School. The story that was told in both the essay and this book are generally the same with similar plot points. However, it went through many changes that became *High-Mount's Champion*.

Now, why I wrote this story in the first place was because I always loved stories about medieval knights who would go on adventures; ranging from rescuing the damsel or to find some treasure or MacGuffin. Either way, if it meant to save the day or to earn fame and fortune, then it was an exciting and heartfelt story. So that was what I wanted to do for myself. However, I noticed that some of those stories were either vain or the main characters didn't aim to do the right thing for the the right thing's sake. To me at least, some of those stories I couldn't help but notice they didn't have God as an active and/or passive part of the story. Or at least have him involved at all. So, that was what I resolved to present in this book.

To do this, I wrote the story to be based on the traditional Hero's Journey and the typical "rescue the damsel" plotline you would see in a lot of fairy tales or medieval stories. I know that such a story can be overdone, and would result in some growing annoyed and longing for something new (which can be understandable when you've see it everywhere 24/7). However, I believe that such a story can be good if the characters felt real and compelling to both the writer and their audience. Most importantly, when telling a story, I learned that it must be told from a place of love and passion, not cynicism and arrogance.

As for the inspirations behind the story, it took me a lot of time playing video games such as *the Legend of Zelda, Sonic the Hedgehog,* and the Zombies mode on *Call of Duty: Black Ops.* In addition, it took reading the Holy Bible and a lot of classic literature ranging from *Sir Gawain and the Green Knight* and Mary Shelley's *Frankenstein* to horror stories ranging from John W. Campbell's *Who Goes There* to H.P. Lovecraft's *The Color out of Space.* With these inspirations in mind, you can say this book was a love letter to the things. A combination of the things I loved both as a kid and as an adult with my Catholic faith at its core.

— · —

ACKNOWLEDGEMENTS

It is commonly belief that a writer creates the story on their own. Of course, this is not true nor is it practical. This story was not written in a vacuum. Instead, I had some help throughout the last seven years in bringing this book to life; from the story's conception to the final version. So, I would like to thank the following people:

To the Lord my God (aka Jesus Christ) for blessing me with the gift of creativity. For without Him, this story would have never been written.

To those in my Church who have given me the honor of being a lector during Mass. With this opportunity, it gave me the confidence needed for presenting this book to the world of literature.

To those in the young adult ministries throughout the Archdiocese of San Antonio who showed interest in this book and all its content.

To my friends. Especially Athalia who helped me brainstorm ideas on how to expand upon some aspects of the story and where to find inspiration for character designs and story layout. To my friends Natalia, Abby, Frida, Anna, Brianna, Andres and Phillip who were willing to listen to me tell the story and present to them the drawings of my characters. Also, a special thanks to Brianna for pointing out that the many errors in the original version published so that I can fix them and re-publish. It was these specific friends who kept on encouraging me to continue writing in general and to finish the book.

To those who have beta-read this story. They helped give me a good idea on how many would react, think about, and enjoy this story.

To my family, especially my mom and my sister Ana who dealt with me constantly babbling on and on about my ideas and this story over the last seven years. To my mom who helped me with the editing and publishing process. To my dad who helped guide me to where I am now so I can have the freedom to write my stories. To my Tio Aaron who was the inspiration behind the name of the main character.

To those who I have sent drafts of the story on Discord and responded with their proper feedback. Without their assistance, I would not have caught a majority of the initial grammatical and story flow errors before publishing. Additionally, their feedback confirmed that this book is objectively a good story outside of the biases of my family and friends.

To those in my creative writing classes back in college. Especially Ava who told me that one of my characters coincidentally shared her sister's name. She too is a fellow writer. Thank you also to a fellow peer Dusty who pointed out some deep meanings behind a lot of the content in the story that I did not think about until it was pointed out to me. Initially I wrote what I wrote because I thought it was cool.

To my English professors back when I was in college. Especiallyo my Creative Writing Professor, Dr. Carstensen, for teaching me about how fun and wonderful creative writing can be. To my British Literature Professor, Dr. Zeman, for sharing *Sir Gawain and the Green* Knight in her British Literature class which explains what inspired this book's writing structure. She also gave a few tips on the historical contexts from this story and what I can do to make my story feel more original, as well as exploring the deeper meanings and historical contexts of such classic stories.

To both Kindle Direct Publishing, Barnes & Noble, and Ingram Spark for giving me the methods to self-publish. Without them, this story may not have been published as it was presented.

Finally, I would like to thank you, the reader, for taking the time to read this book. I hope you enjoyed.

— · —

ABOUT THE AUTHOR

Raymond Herrera is new to the world of fantasy and science fiction. He was diagnosed with Autism and ADHD at a young age which made reading and writing difficult for him. As an adult, he discovered a love for literature after reading Mary Shelley's *Frankenstein* alongside other works of classic literature. He then spent the next few years earning a BA in English from Texas A&M University – Corpus Christi to pursue his newfound passion. As a result, he turned his lifelong love for medieval stories, fairy tales, video games, and his Catholic Faith into written word. When he's not lost in literature or writing, he can be found at Church, at home, or exploring places throughout his hometown of San Antonio, Texas.

www.ingramcontent.com/pod-product-compliance
Lightning Source LLC
Chambersburg PA
CBHW020334010826
48970CB00011B/661